Warriors Arise

Discovering your destiny through those who have gone before you

The Story of the Warriors of Team Xtreme International

Thanks to all my heroes…

- The Father, Son, and Holy Spirit;

- Laura, my lovely wife and lifelong helpmate;

- My world-changing children: Sasha, Savannah, and Michael;

- Amazing TX/SEI/IWT leaders around the world;

- Loren and Darlene Cunningham of Youth With A Mission;

- Mark Anderson of the Impact World Tour;

- Mike Bickle and the International House of Prayer;

- All the forerunners who have made a road before

Table of Contents

Introduction
Kevin Stark

When I was a young believer, and my wife Laura and I were just starting our missionary journey, we loved to listen to the great generals of the faith telling their miracle stories. The stories really built up our faith, but they also stirred up a burning desire in our hearts for these things to happen through us. Since we had no similar God stories of our own, I would often tell others' stories, while dreaming of being used by God in the same way.

One day, the Lord brought me to the story about David, the young shepherd boy, who while still young and unknown, was used by God to kill a lion and a bear. David went on to become the king of Israel and to do great exploits for God. After reading about David the prayer of my heart was, "Thank You, Father, for all these stories of great men, but I want my own lion and bear stories, for your glory!" At first I thought this might be prideful or self-centered, but I discovered that exploits like David's were supposed to be part of a normal Christian lifestyle, and that my desires for exploits are a normal result of living in the Kingdom of God.

This book is about our journey with Team Xtreme and Youth With A Mission. Ultimately, the purpose of this book is to jump-start your journey. Everyone can benefit from reading it, but it is a call especially to men to arise and fulfill their destinies as leaders, fathers, husbands, and world-changers. Too many of God's men have been silenced, seduced, and sedated by the world and the devil, and sometimes even by the church. We have been told to be quiet, to fit in, and not to dream. However, there is in each of us the DNA of a warrior, created by God to co-create with Him, to do great exploits, to go places no person has ever gone before, to do things no one has done before, to rise up and live a life of integrity, purpose, and power.

Many of our Team Xtreme members over the years have been like David's mighty men of the Old Testament—misfits of the world, nobodies, going nowhere, and doing nothing. But when they were transformed by the power of the cross and filled with the Holy Spirit, they began to live out what they were designed to be—warriors serving a mighty king who knows no limits or boundaries.

This book will give you revelation through men who have gone before you that God wants you to live a life where the supernatural is the norm. The testimonies in this book are telling the story of Team Xtreme, but they will also provoke you to believe for your own warrior stories, to break off strongholds and apathy, to give you new vision, and to give you permission to dream again.

This book has many authors who have joined us on our journey to know God and to make Him known. Like David's mighty men, we have fought many hard battles together, standing as one in victory and defeat. Through our battle scars and weakness, we are receiving new revelation of God's Glory, and we are fulfilling our ultimate purpose to become worshiping warriors. Laura and I are honored to have such awesome and amazing friends, and staff with whom to experience the Kingdom of God.

We have written this book with the prayer that the ceiling of our experiences of seeing the power and glory of God will become your floor, your foundation. We pray that you will experience much greater exploits in God than we ever have. We believe we are living in the days of the last generation, who will see the greatest and most amazing harvest the world has ever known, and who will usher in the second coming of Christ.

It is time for some of you to let go of vain imaginations, past hurts and failures, and wrong decisions. It is time for you to take up your sword and your shield, to put on your breastplate of righteousness, belt of truth, and your good new shoes, and to get up on your mighty stallion and ride again. For others of you, it is time to dream bigger dreams with God, to go up higher, to enter into the fullness of your destiny. If God has done it for us, He can do it for each one of you. It is time to get back on your horse and ride.

To our Lord and Savior Jesus Christ be all the glory, honor, and praise

Chapter 1: Sudden Beginning
Kevin Stark

I was about to thrust my forearm through eight concrete blocks that were ablaze with fire, and I looked over at my wife's fear-filled face in the audience. I could read her quivering lips, "What are you doing?" I refocused back to the task before me, to smash a wall of bricks that looked ten feet high and seemed unbreakable. The five hundred people in the gym began to scream, my heart began to pound, and sweat began to pour down my face. I thought, "Jesus, help me." Fears of breaking my arm, or even worse, of making a complete fool of myself, raced through me. I had never done this before, and this was crazy. What was I even doing up here?

Suddenly, there was a shift. For some reason, faith and confidence began to fill me. The crowd began to chant so loud my ears were ringing. I went from thinking, "There is no way I can do this!" To, "This might be possible!" For a moment it seemed like time stood still. It felt like I was in a faith bubble that kept me immune from fear and unbelief. I could hear the crowd, but it seemed like I was alone with God. Could this be the moment I had been waiting for?

Have you ever had the supernatural experience of a thought turning into faith, and then that faith pushing you over the top into action? Well, it was about to happen to me for the first time. Without knowing it, this one step of faith was about to launch my family, myself, and many others into our destiny.

The emcee for the night screamed, "Just hit it hard!" That was the trigger that set my faith in motion. I jumped into the air, and every muscle in my body began to explode. I do not even remember breaking the bricks. It seemed like they just broke as if I had done this hundreds of times before. The crowd went crazy, and for that one moment I was Superman, King Kong, and the Incredible Hulk all wrapped up in one man's body.

4

Just after my moment of fame, God made sure I stayed humble because the first thing I noticed after I broke the bricks was the smell of burning hair. After the show, I looked in the mirror and noticed I had burned my eyelashes, eyebrows, and the front of my hair. The Superhero had a weakness—he burns.

During the outreach that night, I had the amazing opportunity to blow up a hot water bottle, bend a steal bar on my head, and break some bricks that were on fire. However, the most amazing part of the evening was when one hundred fifty people came rushing up to the altar to give their life to Jesus. As I looked down with tears in my eyes, I was so amazed that God allowed me to be a part of this. I could never have imagined that evening that this would be the beginning of seeing hundreds of thousands of people from all over the world make the same choice to follow Christ.

It is important for you to know some of the context of this journey. This brick-breaking moment in time had been preceded by many years of waiting on the Lord, prophetic promises, tests, trials, failures, and breakthroughs. There were seasons in the wilderness and seasons of preparation, including being mentored by faithful men. But this was the day the Lord chose to tap me on my shoulder and say, "It is time." This day was not about me, but about a God who loves to bless and release His children into their Kingdom purposes.

What had brought me to that day? I had been in an organization called Youth With A Mission (YWAM) for several years. The central purpose of their mission is to know God and make Him known. One of the core values of YWAM is to teach each person to hear the voice of the Lord, and to be obedient to whatever the Lord asks them to do. In seeking to live out this value, my family and I were led by the Lord to leave our jobs, our country, our friends and extended family, and by faith, to travel the world to preach the good news of Jesus. The journey was not easy. In fact, in the short term it seemed to cost a lot. But as we began to walk this faith journey out, we learned that with every sacrifice came a blessing. As we learned about dying to self, we also learned there is a resurrection. With every closed door we encountered, we saw that the Father always opened another that was better on the other side. The entryway through the starting gate was narrow, but we discovered the green meadow on the other side of a lifetime of discovery while learning to know and walk with the God who created everything.

We were led into a life of sowing seeds of serving, sacrifice, and obedience, which has turned into a harvest of blessing, revelation, and love.

For several years we served in Asia. Some of our assignments there were very significant and fulfilling, while others were just plain difficult and seemed to be insignificant. However, we knew it was not about making it to the top, but it was about the climb and lessons learned along the way. As we planned our course, the Lord directed our path.

The final step of obedience in our journey to the brick-breaking night was following the Lord's leading our family, from an Olympic coaching job in Hong Kong, to a small YWAM base in Lakeside, Montana. More than just an insignificant assignment, it seemed to become what I called our "season of insignificance". We went from the spotlight of coaching world-class athletes to running intramural basketball games in the rugged mountains. It seemed like a demotion, but God was setting us up to go to a new level.

The Lord had moved us all the way from Hong Kong to Montana just to meet a man named Mark Anderson. Mark was about to start a worldwide evangelism movement called the Impact World Tour. He invited us on the first tour, and our first stop was Turtle Lake, Wisconsin. My assignment for this tour was to conduct sports camps. I completed our first sports camp on a Saturday afternoon in a high school gym—the very gym where our first strong man show would be held on the evening of that same Saturday. A team of three guys was scheduled to perform, but only one guy showed up. At 6:50 p.m., the gym was packed out for the 7:00 pm show, and only one team member was ready to perform. The emcee saw me sitting in the front row. He knew I was part of YWAM, and that I had just conducted the sports camp. In desperation, he called me up to the stage and asked if I could help out. He threw me a shirt, and the music started. The first show of the Impact World Tour had begun.

As I stood on the stage, I had no clue what was going on. I thought I was up there to move broken bricks off the stage. To my total surprise, the emcee, who did not even know my name, announced to the crowd that I was going to blow up a hot water bottle! He then announced another feat of strength, and another. After each announcement, he put down the microphone, turned his head toward me, and screamed out instructions. Then he would put the microphone back to his mouth, turn back to the audience, and get them to scream again.

Can you feel what it would have been like to be me in this situation? It was like pulling the janitor out of the crowd at a football game and putting him into the game as your starting quarterback. I had no experience at this stuff, but the Father in Heaven wanted to give me a gift. He wanted to give it to me in such a unique and sudden way that I knew it was from Him.

Now you know the beginning of the story. This sudden Saturday night surprise turned into a worldwide ministry that has allowed my family and me to preach the gospel in over eighty nations to millions of people. We have seen hundreds of thousands of salvations, healings, and deliverances. My family and I give all the praise, honor and glory to the Lord, and are so grateful to the group of awesome leaders, intercessors, and financial supporters God has provided for us along the way. If God can do it for us, He can do it for you.

Revelation

Discovering your destiny is a lifetime process that becomes clearer as you get more revelation.

Your dreams are from God. Do not get confused by wondering if your dreams are God's will for your life.

There are NO LIMITS to your destiny with GOD, except for the limit of your unbelief.

Be obedient to the next (small?) thing God asks you to do. He is just as interested in each step of the journey as He is in the end results.

Your identity is the key to your destiny. Once you get revelation of who you are you will know where you are to go and what you are to do.

Application

Take a walk with God. Take your Bible with you. Ask Him who you are and what He thinks about you. Write down what He says. You will be surprised.

Chapter 2: From Sniper to Missionary
Marlin Kroeker

The cold hard steel of my MP5 submachine gun pressed against my palms. The smell of the thick underbrush penetrated my nostrils as sweat beaded on my forehead. Camouflaged by my ghillie suit, I slowly crept forward on my stomach to one of the Emergency Response Team (ERT) sniper positions on the east side of the old run down farm house we had surrounded. Inside were believed to be two fugitives, a father and his 19-year old son, both known as the "Talkers", who were wanted for the cold-blooded killing of a police informant only days before. Up to this point, intelligence was unable to pinpoint the location of the men, but we were not taking any chances they were not in the house.

ERT's involvement in the case began several weeks before when six of us had stalked in the darkness in pouring rain to this same house to provide cover for an undercover police officer. Having been in the rain since midnight, our bodies were shivering with cold. We took our positions around the house to provide protection for the officer who was posing as a hit man in an effort to obtain evidence against Talker. It was believed that Talker had murdered his wife. Information had been obtained which claimed that Talker had disposed of her body through a tree shredder onto his fields. This was a cold case that the Royal Canadian Mounted Police (RCMP) was trying to close. The murder of the informant had made the capture of Talker more urgent.

As I lay camouflaged in the undergrowth of the bush surrounding the house, a flicker of what seemed to be light from a television could be seen coming from the large living room window. Since all efforts to make contact with anyone in the house by telephone had failed, the decision was made to throw a stun grenade inside to see if anyone was in there. I watched as the grenade landed in front of a large picture window, knowing the resulting explosion was sure to arouse anyone in the house.

With a tremendous impact the grenade exploded. Within seconds the curtain of the window slowly began to close. My heart rate increased as adrenaline surged through my body knowing that we were now engaged in a standoff with two known killers.

The ensuing standoff lasted thirty-six hours. The mandate of our team was always to resolve a case peaceably, even one of this magnitude. There was no immediate action needed because, to the best of our knowledge, the two men were the only ones in the house. Talker eventually picked up the phone our technicians had connected and spoke to our negotiators, but all efforts to negotiate surrender failed. In fact, the senior Talker had said that we would not take them alive. The situation was critical as Talker had been bragging that he had set up explosive booby traps around his property.

Throughout the standoff we threw in explosive devices, tear gas, and listening devices, but there was no response. Eventually, we had to enter and search the dwelling. Heavily armed, four of us made our way up the narrow stairs. We waited the five minutes it took to make an explosive device we decided to use to break in the door where they had to be. The charge was detonated and the power of the water in the device forced the door in, taking it off the hinges while pushing the items that had barricaded it back. I ran up the stairs with my team leader and entered the room with my submachine gun in ready position.

What we found inside was gruesome and sad. Both Talkers lay on the floor, their rifles draped across their laps, their lives taken by a single self-inflicted gunshot to their heads. They were right when they said that they would not be taken alive. As I looked out the window of the room, I saw where I had been hiding in a sniper position providing cover for hours not long before. I strongly felt God impress on my heart that once again He had been my protection throughout this experience.

My career as a police officer had started about seven years before this event. I was blessed to have been raised in a Christian home. I lived the outward life of a Christian, but did not commit my life completely to Jesus Christ until I had graduated from high school. Until then, I had really been living an idolatrous lifestyle. I worshiped cars and material things, but God was working on my heart.

Eventually, I fully surrendered myself to Him, and immediately began to see that Jesus Christ wanted a relationship with me, and that He had a purpose and a plan for my life. I enrolled in Trinity Western University and pursued a degree in Biblical studies and psychology. I thought that God was leading me either to be a policeman or a preacher.

Before I found out which role He was calling me to fill, I met a wonderful woman named Susan in my last year of college and fell madly in love. God impressed on my heart that Susan was to be my wife, and after just our first date, I went home and told my parents that I had found the girl I was going to marry. We were married in July of 1986. Deuteronomy 24:6 says that a newly married man is not to engage in military activity, but is to stay home and bring happiness to his wife for the first year they are married. We made a covenant before God to spend our first year committed to building a solid foundation for our marriage, and I continued to try to discover what it was God wanted me to do.

During the 1980's, it was very hard to get into the RCMP, and I had begun the application process four years prior. Six months into our marriage I received a call from the recruitment division of the RCMP advising me that they wanted me in training in four weeks. I told them that I was not prepared to go because I was newly married. If I went to training it would mean that Susan and I would be separated for six months, as I would be going to the academy located in another province. I felt sick when I hung up the phone because I thought I had given up an opportunity to be in a career that God seemed to be leading me to. I knew in my heart though that I had to honor the

11

covenant that I had made with my wife and God. We carried on in our jobs and concentrated on building our marriage.

Several months later the phone rang in our small duplex. I picked it up and was surprised to once again hear a recruiter for the RCMP on the phone. He said he had a new date for me, and that date turned out to be within one day of our first year wedding anniversary. There was peace in Susan's and my heart as we knew this was the direction that God was taking us. It also was a confirmation of God's desire for us to honor Him in the covenant of our marriage.

After training, my first post was to a small town called Kamsack in the Province of Saskatchewan. Its nickname was "Little Chicago" because the murder rate was higher per capita than Chicago, Illinois. Kamsack was an obviously exciting place to learn how to police, but still a great location to start a family. We had our three beautiful kids while posted there.

God had other reasons for us to be there too. The town was pretty much dead spiritually, and the only Bible-believing church was nearly empty, but God brought a wonderful pastor and the church began to flourish.

Even with Kamsack's benefits there was one thing lacking, and that was the ability to pursue my desire to become a member of the Emergency Response Team (ERT). I had been asking God to put us near the city of Regina because of the ERT based there, and after four and a half years He led us out of Kamsack through a transfer to Regina. It was not long after we were transferred that I received the training and became a member of the ERT. During my three years on the team, I received extensive training in special weapons and techniques (SWAT), including sniper training, and was deployed in many different situations.

After eight years with the RCMP—filled with diverse experiences that brought growth and national pride—Susan and I felt God leading us to the city of Medicine Hat in the Province of Alberta where I joined the police force. At the time we wanted stability for our family, but we were to learn later that God had other purposes for clearly leading us to this city where I had a great career of ten years as a police officer. I served on the SWAT team of the department in the positions of Assaulter, Sniper, Team Leader, and Commander of the team. I also was able to become part of the Technical Section and the Recruitment Team, served as a detective for several years, and was promoted to the rank of Sergeant.

After 18 years, first as a member of the RCMP and then as a part of the Medicine Hat Police Service, God's call to ministry was still on our lives. Though I felt that while serving as a police officer I was right where God wanted me, as the years progressed I felt a stronger and stronger pull towards ministry. I had been in many dangerous situations, even life-threatening ones, but my heart's desire was always to serve and follow the Lord Jesus Christ. I didn't realize it then, but my time as a police officer was preparation for what God had in store for me. The desire to preach the gospel had never left me. We have since learned that God puts His desires in our hearts, but it may take years before He actually wants us to step into them. He is always working to develop our character and to fulfill His purposes in our lives as we surrender control.

In 2002, Impact World Tour (IWT) came to our city to hold a series of crusades. Our family was excited about this event and involved in its planning. It was to be held in our city's ice arena, and my role was to organize and provide security for the event. Although working as a detective at the time, I put on my uniform again and did my job. The performances were exciting, but it was most thrilling of all to see the many people that went forward to receive the gift of salvation through Jesus Christ.

During one of the team lunches at a local church, I met Kevin Stark, the leader of Team Xtreme International. One of the team members who was nearby asked, what seemed to me as a joke, if I wanted to become part of Team Xtreme. I had been weight training since I was eighteen years old, but I really didn't feel that I fit the bill. I didn't think I could perform the feats of strength that the team was doing, and the thought of performing was definitely out of my comfort zone, but a seed had been planted.

Prior to the evangelistic events, there was a planning meeting for all the churches that would be participating. One of the IWT leaders of the meeting asked if there was anyone who wanted to go and help with an upcoming crusade to India. Our daughters, Katie-Lee, Jana-Marie, and our son Davis were each sitting in different locations in the arena, but all of us felt the call to go and we all stood to our feet. There was excitement in our van as we drove home talking about this step of faith we had taken together that evening, but it seemed impossible.

At the time, we were building our dream home on some acreage outside the city. Susan had been staying at home while schooling the kids. Living on one income, we had no extra money to go on this $14,000 trip, but we knew God was calling us. With fearful first steps we started raising the finances.

We learned very quickly that God loves our steps of faith. One incident in particular helped solidify our understanding of our position in Christ, and to know more of His heart for us. The missions trip was to commence in November, and we needed $7,300 by the middle of October to pay for the plane tickets. The team had been working hard to raise the money through bake sales, other group fundraising activities, and seeking out the support of individuals. As a family, we had raised about $6,000. I was working a side renovation job on a 4-plex that we hoped would be completed in time to cover the cost, but we were nowhere near finished. (God had other plans for that property we found out later.)

On the morning the money was due, I got a call from the IWT office telling me that someone had donated $550 to our family's cause, but we still needed $730. I went to work that day on the 4-plex filled with faith that God was going to bring in the money. At noon, I drove to the post office anticipating an envelope with a donation. As I opened our post office box my heart was flooded with disappointment—it was completely empty. Heavy-hearted, I went to the missions office and wrote a check on my Visa account. I knew that God did not want us to go into debt to pay for this trip—we had discussed this as a family—but I felt I had no other option.

I drove the six miles home in quiet contemplation and prayer wondering what I would tell our three young kids, especially since we had been praying and fasting as a family throughout the day for the answer. Susan and our three excited kids met me when I walked in the back door asking if I had heard the news. My first response was to tell them I had heard that someone had given us a gift of $550 dollars. I wanted to hide my disappointment in what I thought was God not coming through for us.

Was I ever wrong! The kids told me we had received a call from the airlines telling us they had overcharged us for our two youngest children by $730, the exact amount we had been short! There was great joy in our house as we praised God for His provision! Our faith in God's desire and ability to provide rose to a new level as we saw Him provide more than enough for us to go on the trip.

The mission trip to India was the start of a fantastic journey of God's leading, providing, and directing us as a family into full-time missions. Our paradigm of faith was blown apart as we saw God cause the deaf to hear, the sick to be healed, the demon-oppressed to be delivered, and most importantly, people coming to faith in Jesus Christ. We came back wrecked from this trip—in a good way—as God in His faithfulness started us on a journey of drawing closer to Him and of fulfilling His call on us for full-time ministry. The same call He had placed on our lives years before.

Even with the dramatic jump-start to fulfilling the call on our lives that this trip provided, the transition into full-time ministry was still a process. We discovered once again that God is a God of mercy, who is faithful, and gently leads with love and grace. When we got home, we felt that we would put a fleece out to see if we were to pursue missions. The fleece came in the form of an application for a ten-month leave of absence from the Police Department. We believed in our hearts that if God wanted us to do this trip He would have the department grant the leave. In human terms, the chances were slim, given the resource needs of the department, but they granted us the leave.

Many felt that we were crazy to embark on a ten-month mission trip. We had no money for this, and we owned acreage that would need to be sold or rented. Besides, I was putting my position as a police officer at risk, but at the same time our family was growing with excitement at where God was taking us. The 4-plex I was working on for the past eight months was getting close to being finished. Not knowing how much it was worth or would sell for, we were pleasantly surprised when the profit was double what we had anticipated. It was almost the exact amount we would need to pay for our plane tickets and the YWAM Discipleship Training School in Kona, Hawaii, we had applied for. The tickets would allow us to stop in Hawaii for the school, and then carry on to New Zealand where we would team up with Team Xtreme and Impact World Tour scheduled to evangelize across the entire nation.

God was showing us that He is able to do much more than we can ever hope or imagine, even when we think we have made a mistake. When we were planning our trip we had booked all the stops on our tickets according to the corresponding dates we were to be in different locations. Two weeks after we set the dates we found out that the tour in New Zealand would be starting two months later then we had initially been told. Our first response was to panic, but then it became clear that God wanted us to go on the two-month outreach phase of

16

our Discipleship Training School, which included travel to Hong Kong, China, and then to the Philippines.

The cost for this trip was $14,000 U.S. With the exchange rate this amounted to $20,000 in Canadian currency—money that we did not have. Again, in faith, we stepped out to believe God for the finances. As soon as we made this commitment, an envelope was handed to us with $800 U.S. dollars in it. On Susan's birthday another anonymous envelope was handed to us containing $2,000 U.S. We continued to believe as a family that God would provide the finances, but on the day we needed the money, we were short $11,000.

The cost for the whole team was $45,000 dollars. It was written on the chalkboard at the front of our classroom and seemed to scream out how much was needed for all of us to go on the mission trip. Our family's need of $11,000 looked gigantic in comparison to the other students' needs. Susan and I had some cash in our bank account set aside for spending money, but even though it wasn't much, we felt we should give a portion of it. After praying we agreed that God wanted us to give $1,000. On a break, I paid this amount, and as soon as I got back I was surprised to see our amount on the blackboard had gone down to $8,000! We rejoiced and remained confident that God would meet the total amount with just a few hours remaining.

Just before noon the class watched in anticipation as the person in charge of finance walked up to the chalkboard. Excitement mounted as one by one each amount was crossed out and replaced with zeros. There was much rejoicing as once again God had met the entire need of our class, including our family's $11,000 dollar shortfall!

What an awesome experience it was to share Christ in the nations of China and the Philippines. In New Zealand, we saw over 27,000 people come forward to give their lives to Christ during the Impact World Tour outreach. We had little money left after we paid for our plane tickets and schooling, yet God faithfully provided for us the whole way. He even provided reliable renters for our acreage. God is faithful.

Upon returning to Canada, the call of God for our lives was clear, but we still struggled with the thought of leaving my career—our earthly security and source of income up to this point. I pleaded with God that if He wanted me to stay with the police force He would give me passion for it, but my heart was always to do ministry. After fourteen months we made the decision for me to resign. I broke down and cried after resigning knowing that I had given up a big part of my life, but God comforted and assured me that He would provide for our family.

In January of 2006, we launched into full-time ministry by starting Team Xtreme Canada. The road has not been easy, but it has been amazing. God has proven Himself over and over. His Word is true and can be completely trusted. He has called us to travel to different nations to preach the gospel, and has been incredibly faithful to provide for our every need.

My career as a police officer was exciting and fulfilling in many ways, but as I look back I can honestly say that I would not change God's direction in my life for anything. By stepping out in faith I have learned that God's heart is not to put us in a box. He really does have good plans for our lives, and often these plans are nothing like what we think they are. God has shown us over and over that He is faithful and wants us to step out in faith. Our family has so many stories of God's provision and blessings on this journey. There is no place I would rather be than in His will because it is a place of abundance. I am fulfilling what He wants me to do, and there is no greater joy than to be in His will, living for His Kingdom, no matter what the circumstances.

Revelation

Your preparation is a key part of your destiny.

God can use every experience in your past for the fulfillment of your future.

Do not despise the day of small beginnings.

Often the first step of faith will be the most difficult.

Many times there will be death of a vision before there is a resurrection of your destiny.

Application

Write down your life vision. Remember, your vision is your dream manifested 10-20 years from now.

Chapter 3: Bram's Supernatural Provision
Bram Buirenhuis

I joined Team Xtreme in the first part of 2002. Right from the beginning of, I had a great interest in seeing the things from the Bible happen in our day. The desire for the supernatural really began in my YWAM Discipleship Training School outreach. God had used me to see many miracles during that training, and I decided the supernatural lifestyle was going to be normal the rest of my life.

As I began working with Team Xtreme, I soon found out that, while my views were sometimes the exception on the team, they were often especially the exception in the church. It seemed that many in the church did not believe the things I believed, and that they were not too interested in changing those beliefs either. There was often great resistance to the supernatural, so I decided simply to seek God and His power and to trust Him that the doors would open. Through the years that is exactly what I have seen happen. The more miracles and supernatural things that took place, the more interesting it became for me, and the more interested people became who were skeptical at first.

Once, when our team was in New Zealand, I had a teammate who was convinced that the gifts of the Spirit had ceased with the first century apostles. After our show I asked him to come with me to pray for people. A non-Christian man came up to us who said, "If your God can heal, can He take this ball off my foot?" As we looked at his foot, we saw a tumor that looked like a ball, and it was hard like a bone. I asked my Team Xtreme teammate, who didn't believe in the gifts of the Spirit, to lay his hand on the ball on this man's foot while we prayed. Within seconds, the non-Christian man fell to the floor, and my teammate was freaking out.

My teammate said, "I felt that ball disappear right under my hand!" The man that fell down woke up, and I asked him what had happened. He said, "I saw angels and flew with them." He got up and asked how he could become a Christian. We led him to the Lord, and he went on the stage and testified that he had just met Jesus. He said that he got saved, healed of the growth on his foot, and flew with angels. My teammate changed his mind too, and began to believe that God had not stopped doing cool things.

There are other examples. One of the biggest moments that brought breakthrough for the supernatural in the Impact World Tour campaigns was the time we were in Holland praying for non-Christian people on the stage. We saw the power of God hit them, and as a result they gave their lives to Jesus. Also, when we were in Denmark, God gave me a word of knowledge about a girl. He gave me her name and all kinds of details about her life. After the show, she came up to the front and wanted to give her life to Jesus. The next day the local newspaper in that Danish city had an article in it with the headline, "Strongman Show Turns Into Revival."

God didn't just move supernaturally on the stage, but we also saw Him work miracles of provision in our everyday lives. I had the privilege of taking along many individuals with me to pray for people on trips, and because of this I began to desire to train others in the supernatural. I really wanted to see a difference in the people I ministered with, and to. When I moved to Brazil, I began to feel compassion for the sick and poor. I was confronted with them every day, and God began to put them on my heart. We started to work with not just the poor, but also with the gangs, drug dealers, addicts, and prisoners. My desire was to see God change those whom the world had given up on.

The desire to train people in the supernatural, and the desire to minister to the poor and outcast, meant we needed a place where we could combine the training and ministry in a better way—even if it meant having the people live with us. At that time, we lived at the Impact World Tour YWAM Base, and there wasn't a desire to mix those people in with the families on the base.

We started to look around for property and found a farm on the Internet. Sheldrey, my wife, and I drove to the farm and walked around the property. We both had the same thought—this was not for us. It was very big and not everything was finished. We left, but during the night, we both started feeling like it was the place after all. We went back to the property and prayed over the area. We told the owners we were interested and went back home dreaming about our supernatural training center.

We didn't have the money to buy the farm, but we felt the Lord telling us that this was it. After a short time we got a phone call telling us the owners had left the farm, and they wanted to rent it out. We called to tell them we wanted to rent it. After they told us the price, I said we would pay a third of that. He refused the offer, but I told him I would visit him the next day.

I arrived early in the morning and asked him if he had changed his mind. He looked at me and asked, "What are you going to do with this farm?" I told him it would be a place to train people in evangelism and the supernatural, and that we wanted to help the poor and eventually bring orphans into our home. He then completely reversed himself and told me we could rent it for the one-third price I had offered the day before. He told me that the night before, just after we had first talked, he had a dream. He saw this place full of young people and children he had never seen before! Within a week we had moved in, and right away, God told us to buy the property. We signed a rent-to-buy contract instead of just a rental agreement, and the next day we left for the USA.

While in the US, we started to share our vision and the story of how we moved to the farm with twelve months to rent, and that we would have to buy the farm at that point. Some people told me I was crazy, but many joined in and began to pray with us. We needed 300,000 Brazilian Realis (the plural of Real—pronounced Ray-al—is like our dollar), which was then $230,000 in US dollars, but within weeks the Real dropped in value. We figured God had raised about half of the budget since R$300,000 was now only $120,000 US. Our faith was growing stronger as we tried to raise the money. Slowly enough money came in to keep us on the farm. As the funds came, we would pay the owner.

One day I was getting really frustrated at the slow pace of the fundraising, so I went for a ride and was worshiping God in the car. While I was listening to a preaching by Larry Randolph, Mr. Randolph stopped his message and said, "You are having difficulty in raising the money for this property and you are worried, but God said He will give you more than enough, and even the lands around you are yours." I drove home totally excited and told Sheldrey what had happened. She said, "Just do not tell anybody because they will think you are strange!"

Within a few days, my neighbor came and asked me to keep an eye on his land, and he gave me the key. It was not our land, but I was able to walk on it and pray. God decided to confirm that word from Larry Randolph, and three different times He used a prophet to tell me that the land around us was ours too. When our rental contract was over, the owner wanted the full amount for buying the farm. We still did not have it, but within a week a large amount of money came in, including a gift from an older man who sold his gold collection and sent us a check for $20,000 US.

We were so excited! We had enough for a down payment, and we took it to the owner. He accepted the down payment and gave us another six months to raise the rest of the money! Unfortunately, during those six months, the Real went up again, and the total purchase price had grown to over $170,000 US. We needed even more money, but at least the exchange rate did not change again. For about five months we prayed and waited, but nothing happened.

While I was in the US, I spoke at the International House of Prayer in Kansas City at a meeting of the evangelism community there. They prayed for me after I spoke, and during this prayer time, a woman prophesied in detail about the farm in Brazil and how people would give us money and laid it at my feet. She even described how they would come with gold, just like the older man had done. This was really a faith booster for me!

Still, after going back to Brazil, nothing happened for quite a while. I asked God what sins I had in my life and what was wrong with me. Did I really hear His voice? People around me started to question it as well, asking things like, "Are you doing everything you can?" "Are you in sin?" "Did you really hear God's voice?" At the very moment I felt like I was the only one left in this battle, I received a message from somebody asking how much we still needed to pay for the farm. He said that God had told him to ask me that. I went to Sheldrey and told her that God did not forget us. While we were arranging the last few documents for our non-profit, God moved! The day we opened our bank account for the organization we received an anonymous donation of R$150,000! It felt like winning the lottery, and I screamed for joy! Now we only needed R$42,000 to pay off the rest of the purchase price. As a final faith booster, God had spoken to the Director of Team Xtreme, Kevin Stark, and some others, that the Lord would pay it in full that year.

I called the homeowner and offered him the money we had in-hand—even though we were R$42,000 short—believing that he would take the smaller amount. When I told him the offer, he started to get a little mad, so we decided to meet face-to-face. When we met he immediately started to say we were late and that we needed to pay interest. I looked at him, and said, "The only reason I am buying your land is because God told me to." I also told him that God had said it would be paid in full before the end of the year, even though it was already December 29. As I was speaking to him, he started to shake like he had Parkinson's disease. Even my lawyer noticed. He was looking through his papers shaking like crazy when he said, "Okay, forget about the interest, and meet me again the first week of January."

The very next day, on December 30, we received a call that the R$42,000 had come in! We called the farm owner and told him that God had done what He said He would do. The next day, as I was talking with Sheldrey, I told her, "This next year I will not do any crazy faith thing! We will just rejoice in this victory."

But God had other plans! By the second week of the New Year, my neighbor came and asked me to rent his property, buy it later, or even to buy it right away. I felt God was in this, so we signed a new contract to rent his farm and buy it afterwards. After we signed the contract, he said, "Hey, the guy next to me wants to sell his land. Do you want it?"

When God has a plan He will make it work. He didn't give us a year's break. I believe it is because He is on a schedule. He is coming and wants us to stick with His timing to finish His work before His return.

Revelation

If your vision can be accomplished through your own ability and resources, it is probably not a God vision.

Vision and destiny involve risk and obedience.

Your destiny will connect with who you are—your pain, your gifts, your abilities, and your passions.

Often times there is a waiting period when you're at the end of all your resources, followed by the sudden provision of God.

Offense and unbelief often shuts down your vision.

Application

Write down all the times you doubted God.

If you had a dream that was aborted because of lack of provision, faith, fear, or doubt of others, write it down.

Repent of any time you doubted God, or any time you were offended by others.

Ask God to close any doors of disappointment, fear, or unbelief that could hinder or stop your vision or dream. Ask God to help you start dreaming again.

Chapter 4: Get Up and Walk
R. K. Castillo

As I walked into my small youth group room, I was greeted by a giant of a man from New Zealand, named Jason, who was part of a presentation to our youth group by Team Xtreme. While I watched, I had a sense that this was what I was supposed to do with my life. At the time, I had no idea I would travel the world with this team and see hundreds of miraculous healings. I was surely in for a big surprise.

In the middle of the show, they asked for a volunteer to get up and embarrass himself in trying to rip up a phonebook. I got up, and of course, I couldn't do it! Kevin Stark then sent me to the back of the room where the big guy showed me how to do it, and I returned to the front of my youth group and amazed them all with my phonebook ripping skills. That night, I went back to watch as they broke bricks, bent bars, and did all the power demonstration stuff. I knew for sure that evening that Team Xtreme was what I was supposed to do. I approached the members of the team and asked them how to sign up.

They told me that I had to go to a school, and if I successfully completed it, I could officially become a member of Team Xtreme. Four months later, I was on my way to Atwater, California, for what they call a "DTS". I had no idea what a DTS was, or YWAM, or any other acronyms for that matter, but this five-month long school totally changed my life. (I found out later "DTS" stands for Discipleship Training School, and "YWAM" stands for Youth With A Mission.)

My time in the DTS was my first experience of hearing stories of how Jesus still comes and changes people's lives right here and right now. In the school, I read stories of Jesus healing people and setting them free, but I never thought I would actually get to see it happen. Wow, was I ever wrong!

After the five-month school session was over, I went back home to Albuquerque and back to my old way of life. I was working at a water park at the time, and one day I got into a huge argument with my girlfriend at work. Just to calm down, I walked to the top of a hill and sat down never expecting what was going to happen next. I do not know how to explain it very well, but in an instant I saw how every person I had loved had hurt me at some time in my life, but I also saw how Jesus was there for me every single time I got hurt. He was the only person who was 100% faithful to me all the time! I sat there in awe of how amazing Jesus was, and I said to Him, "If that is how You really are, I am going to serve You the rest of my life." When I walked down that hill I was a different person. Everywhere I went I would say, "It is just Jesus and me!" It did not matter what was happening, He was with me all the time!

Just two months later, I found myself on a plane to Brazil on my first overseas missions trip with Team Xtreme. We ended up in Londrina, Brazil, for an Impact World Tour (IWT) event. As usual with IWT, we began by performing a couple of school assemblies each day to promote the big show we would do in a stadium a couple of weeks later. The big night came, and we were setting up for the show. It was a pretty hectic setup since our materials had still not arrived just an hour before our first show at the stadium was to start! Everything worked out though, and we did two shows our first night.

At the end of every show, we usually have someone ask those who want to turn control of their lives over to Jesus to respond by coming to the front of the stage. That night was no different, and as the people who came forward were standing in the front, I noticed a man who was doing some weird things. I began to sense that he had a problem with alcohol, and that he needed to be set free. The local pastors took the man to the side, so I had to find him in order to pray for him. When I found him, I asked him what was going on, and he said, "The Devil is trying to kill me."

I replied, "How is he trying to do that?"

"I am an alcoholic," he said.

28

As we began to pray, he immediately began to act crazy. He was trying to punch and kick us, and all kinds of things like that. It was an evil spirit that was tormenting this man. I had never cast out demons before, and my friend and I did the only thing we knew to do. We yelled at the demon and commanded it to leave. Just then, a pastor came over to help us. He actually jumped on the man and began speaking to the evil spirit. He asked the spirit its name, and the spirit answered back through the man's mouth! I had never seen anything like this before. Even though I had read about it in the Bible, I never thought it would actually happen right in front of my eyes.

The pastor called the spirit by name and commanded it to leave. You could see the man's entire countenance change. He looked like a completely different person. We stood him up and asked him his name. It was a completely different name than the one he had told us earlier. I knew then it was the spirit talking through him at first. After ministering to this man and watching him be delivered from an evil spirit, we went back to where we were staying. We were very excited and in awe of how great Jesus really is!

The next night was equally fun. We were walking around during the response time trying to find people to pray for when we walked up to two of our friends who were praying for a ten-year old boy. The boy could not walk because he had blown out both of his knees in sports. A thought came into my mind, "He is not going to get healed sitting on the ground. Stand him up!"

I picked the young man up and spoke into his ear, "Jesus already paid for you to be healed, so I am going to let go of your arms, and you are going to land on the ground. It might hurt at first, but Jesus is going to heal you." I let go of his arms, watched as he landed on the ground, and ran off to his mom completely healed!

There were many amazing things God did during that trip. Everything we prayed for God would make happen. He opened deaf ears and caused paralyzed people to walk. We prayed for one girl that got hit by the power of God, and she was literally lifted off the ground and flew back a couple of feet. Another woman came under the power of God in a parking lot and ended up lying in a puddle from the rain wearing a nice white silk blouse. My friends said I should put something under her head, but I told them everything would be okay. When we helped her up, she was completely clean and totally dry!

God even created money in one of our wallets! My friend and I liked to eat at an amazing potato restaurant in the mall. We were about to leave the town, so it was going to be the last time we could eat there. We checked our wallets and had nothing, but we still went to the mall with our friends. When we got to the food court my friend pulled out his wallet and found fifty dollars! I believe God put it in there for us to have some potatoes! Seeing God do all these miracles, signs, and wonders right in front of me changed my life forever!

Even so, I had some lessons to learn. Two months after we got back from Brazil I heard that Impact World Tour was going to make a trip to India. They told me miracles came easy in India, so I was really excited about this trip after what happened in Brazil. The first night of our show a mother brought me her four-year old daughter. The little girl had a withered hand and her mom wanted to see her healed. I prayed, and prayed, and prayed, but nothing happened. I left that night discouraged, depressed, and defeated, and never wanted to pray for the sick again.

A couple days later, one of the fellows that was traveling with us noticed I was not doing well and asked what was going on. I told him how the little girl was not healed, and that I thought it was my fault. He looked right at me and said, "It is not up to you when they get healed, and it is not your fault when they do not get healed. Your job is to pray and let God do the healing." That made total sense! I went out with a new passion for seeing people healed, and immediately began seeing miracles happen.

On the last night of our ministry, we were out praying for the people when the police blew their whistles and began making their way toward us. In India, they do crowd control differently than we do in the United States. They hit people with sticks and other things just to get them to do what they want them to do. At 9:00 every night during our shows the police would blow their whistles and start making people leave. Right at that time on the last night, a group of fellows brought me their friend, who had two withered hands, and asked me to pray for him. The first thing that came to my mind was, "I could not get a little girl with one withered hand healed earlier this week. How am I going to pray for two withered hands now?" I suddenly remembered it was not my job to heal. It was my job to pray and let God do the healing.

I put my hand on the man's head and prayed, "God, I do not have time to pray, so You are going to have to do what You do right now in the name of Jesus." Immediately, both of his hands shot out! You should have seen the man's face when both of his hands were straightened!

I asked his friends, "What could he not do?" They said, "He cannot grab things." I stuck out my finger and told him to squeeze it. He did, and then I said, "Now get out of here before the cops come and beat you up!"

Since that time, we have seen thousands of people healed and delivered. In Matthew 10:7-8 Jesus says, "As you go, preach this message: the Kingdom of Heaven is near. Heal the sick, raise the dead, cleanse those who have leprosy, drive out demons. Freely you have received, freely give." Healing the sick and seeing miracles is a normal part of the Christian life. It is not optional. I pray that you will go out with a new boldness. May this verse in Mark be true of your life: "These signs shall follow those who believe: in my name they will cast out demons... and they will place their hands on the sick and they shall recover." (Mark 16:16-18)

Revelation

Faith grows as we work it out.

Knowledge without experience is just religion.

Every Kingdom destiny should include the supernatural

God commands us to lay hands on the sick and they will be healed. You don't receive the credit when they get healed, and you do not get the blame when they don't.

Application

Attach yourself to a supernatural culture or mentor.

Read through the Gospels and Book of Acts, highlighting all miracles.

Get some training in healing and miracles.

Ask God for forgiveness for believing that healing was just for the apostles, or that He brings sickness on people to discipline them and to build their character.

Chapter 5: Supernatural Airplane Ticket
Alefosio and Lynn 'Aho

When Kevin Stark told us to pray about the events our team would do in 2008, we sensed that we were to complete what we had started by continuing to participate in the Impact World Tour (IWT) events in Australia. The Lord had told us to invest in the land when we first prayed about whether to join the TX team going to the IWT event in Geraldton, Australia in Feb 2006. 'Ale in particular had a heart for youth and indigenous people in Australia since he had lived in Sydney for several years during his teens, and had succumbed to the many influences that pull young men away from God there.

We wanted to help show others truth and help them get out of spiritual darkness. So we committed to join the IWT events in Australia, traveling from our home in the Kingdom of Tonga. In 2007, we participated in two tours–Townsville and Perth. When we prayed about 2008, it seemed right to continue to invest in the "great south land of the Holy Spirit" (Australia) by joining the tour to Cape York in the northernmost part of the continent.

Our previous trips to IWT in Australia began with just the two of us in 2006. When our son was born later that year, we took him along in 2007. The Lord had added two more young men to our team by 2008. We have always felt that our team was to function as "family", so we knew that all five of us would travel together to the Cape York tour. Our team began praying into the tour, asking God to give us His heart for the indigenous people we would meet. We asked for the strategies to see them released from the kingdom of darkness, and for the Holy Spirit to anoint us with His power to draw people to Himself. We also began praying for the finances we would need for four airline tickets. Thankfully, our son was still under two years old and could travel free of charge. We live on what the Lord provides, and though we had some regular support from a small group of faithful friends, it was not enough to include such an expense!

The two new guys with us on our team had no regular support, but were living by seeing the Lord bring in what they needed, even things like hand and laundry soap, plus some money here and there—they praised the Lord for all of it! The four Tongans (all except Lynn, an American), would need to apply for visas to Australia. The visa situation for Tongans wanting to go to Australia is still not good, and it was not an automatic process. Visa applications for young Tongan males are often rejected due to the abuses of others who have gone before and overstayed. Australian Immigration looks at the applications of young Tongan males with great scrutiny because of this.

We asked Julie McLaughlin, the tour organizer, to rally prayer support for us. After one such prayer time, she communicated to us that the group had sensed the Lord say, "Then suddenly He (God) acted." We were really encouraged! Somehow we knew that God would move quickly, but did not think the word was about finances.

We began doing "the possible"—doing some carwashes to raise money, selling peanuts and barbequed lunches, and being frugal with the money we had. We also started faith prayer walks to the airport, a twenty-five minute walk from our house, to proclaim our trust in the Lord to provide our visas and tickets. We walked several times a week singing and praising God, listening to Him and asking Him to give us His heart for those we would meet and minister to. About a month before the tour was to begin in Cape York, we finally had the money we needed for the four visas and lodged our applications with the Australia High Commission in our capital town, Nuku'alofa. We then checked our finances for airlines tickets and had nearly enough for just one ticket.

We knew we were to travel as a team, and we knew that just in case the visas were NOT granted, we should not purchase any tickets until the visas came through. We just kept walking and claiming our visas since the Creator of the Universe, the King of Kings, had already given us authority to GO into Australia on His business (Matthew 28:19-20).

Within two weeks of our intended departure, we had enough money for just one ticket. We kept contacting the Australia High Commission, even though they frown on that, to check on the status of our visa applications. We were told over and over to wait, and that it would take fourteen business days to process. While waiting, we kept walking to the airport, picking up both our pace and our level of THANKSGIVING BY FAITH that we all would get visas and money for the airline tickets from Tonga to Townsville, Australia. This was the city of our starting point, and from where we would drive for two and a half days to the northernmost area of Australia where the tour would be.

The cheapest airline tickets were quickly being purchased, and since we wanted to be faithful with the money that God had provided, we had some decisions to make. Should we buy one ticket with the money we had to avoid having to pay MORE once the economy tickets were gone? Should we buy that ticket by faith, trusting that the visa would be granted? There could be no refund of the ticket once we purchased it at that price. If money suddenly came in for the other tickets, was it OKAY to travel on a different airline if the cheaper one was already full?

Going back to the word of the Lord to GO to Australia, we decided to purchase the one ticket we had money for, in the name of 'Ale our team leader, and trust that God would also grant his visa to Australia. After calling again to check the progress on the visa, and being told again to "wait", we bought the ticket for a flight one week from that day.

A couple of days later, we decided to go in person to check the visas. This was on a Friday, and 'Ale's ticket was scheduled for the following Monday. 'Ale was told that our visa applications, which had been "lodged" about a month before that day, had not even been considered yet! ("Lodged" is the word they use in Australia while Americans might say the application was "turned in" or something like that.) He was told that our applications had been superseded by groups that applied for immediate visas to attend family funerals in Australia! Tongan culture is such that when someone dies overseas, everyone in the family goes to the funeral—it's a big deal. The custom in Tonga is that visa applications for government personnel and for funerals get first priority. It seemed like death was getting precedence over our venture to bring Jesus' LIFE! 'Ale was told to return at 8:30 on Monday morning to check again if our visas had been processed. His flight was scheduled to leave at 10 a.m.!

We knew what God had said. We knew that we were all supposed to go together as a team and as a family. We knew that we did not have visas for Australia, nor money to buy the remaining three airline tickets. BUT GOD SAID, and that was our declaration as we walked the next day, a Saturday, to the airport. On Sunday night, we gathered again to seek the Lord to be sure that it really was Him saying that we were all to go. We wanted to allow for the possibility that we had "heard wrong", and to give Him an opportunity to correct us, or for Him to encourage us to move ahead. As we prayed, we sensed God confirm that we had "heard right", that we were to continue "walking ahead", and that all of us should pack our suitcases and prepare to leave the next morning at 10:00 on the same flight as 'Ale, even though none of us, not even 'Ale, had visas yet. Besides that, three of us had no tickets!

God gave us the story from Acts 16:25-26, which tells of when Paul and Silas were in prison, and at about midnight they were singing and praising God... Then SUDDENLY... The prison shook and the chains came off! We knew that God wanted us to do the same, and that no matter what—tickets and visas or not—we were to praise Him just for who He is. He would "shake" whatever was holding us back in what He had instructed us to do in Australia. We decided as a team that we would ALL go to the airport in the morning to check in before the scheduled 10 a.m. departure. 'Ale would go early to the Australian High Commission and check on our visas, but we would be prepared!

So, 'Ale went to bed, but I (Lynn) stayed up to start packing for their family of three. After packing 'Ale's things in one suitcase—in case he had to go alone or on a different flight—I sat down and momentarily let myself think that my job was finished, but a bit of doubt crept in. I looked at my watch at 11:50 p.m. What had God said from the passage in Acts? Start praising and thanking Him "about midnight". I began to open my mouth and do just that. It did not make much sense in the natural, but it was not from the natural that the answer would come! In the little room just a few yards away from our house, our team members, Suli and 'Alipate, also started singing. There in the darkness I could hear that they were also singing and packing. I got up again and started putting together another suitcase for me and our twenty-two month old Fungani. "God, I trust you. I have no idea HOW you will do this, but I will be prepared!"

'Ale was up before dawn and in the car on the way to town to the Australian High Commission Office before 7:00 a.m. The office opened at 8:30 a.m. It was a twenty-five minute drive from the house to the town, and he wanted to be the first in line when the doors opened.

When the office opened, he was indeed the first to the window. The woman who had talked with us so many times before smiled, reached under the counter, and produced all five passports neatly rubber-banded together.

"Your visas are inside. Have a good trip."

These were her only remarks! Just to be sure, 'Ale quickly opened the passports. All five visas had been stamped with a one-time visitor's visa for three months which was long enough for the tour! WOW... SUDDENLY... We took the first step.

He quickly called me to tell me the visas were granted, jumped in the car just sixty minutes before departure for the thirty-minute drive to the airport, and told me to have everyone meet him at the airport. Suli and 'Alipate headed to the airport with bags already in another car and met 'Ale, who walked into the check-in, leaving the boys outside to pray. 'Alipate took 'Ale's car to go pick up Fungani and me from home, a five-minute drive, and to bring us to the airport. Along the way, 'Alipate let the YWAM base leadership know that the visas had been granted, and thanked them for their prayers—adding that they could continue to pray for the money needed to buy the three remaining airline tickets.

While all of this was going on, an Australian man visiting the YWAM base heard some noise in the campus chapel and went to investigate. He walked in on the DTS staff and students praying earnestly.

"...and God, please bring in their airline tickets and encourage them as they wait outside the airport."

"Who is waiting at the airport?", he asked.

The DTS leader kind of ignored him, wanting her staff to rise up and answer their own prayers by giving a sacrificial offering to the team. But the man kept asking, so the DTS leader finally answered him that there were four people, including a not quite two-year-old, standing outside the airport waiting on God to bring them their plane tickets to go for an evangelistic outreach to Cape York, Australia.

"God's people should not have to stand outside like that!", he exclaimed, and asked that he be driven immediately to the airport.

The DTS leader found a car, and telephoned me as I waited outside the airport with Fungani and the two boys.

"I am on my way to the airport with someone who wants to give you money for your tickets!", she explained excitedly.

I started screaming, crying, and jumping up and down… Could it be? Really? Was this the "suddenly" that we were expecting? And who is this mystery donor?

I expected to see some dignitary or the Princess coming out of the car. Instead, Jesus came walking up to me in the "skin" of an Australian pensioner with a long white beard, somewhat disheveled in appearance, but carrying the heart of God for the Aboriginal people of his land.

"How much do you need?", he asked.

He started shuffling through his belt pack looking for his bank card. We directed him to 'Ale, who was waiting in the queue to check-in.

"How much do you need?", he asked 'Ale again.

So many thoughts passed through 'Ale's mind. Who is this man? Does he know that there are three people who need tickets? Where did he come from?

We had never talked to him. Calmly, 'Ale explained that three people standing outside the airport were praying and trusting God for their airline tickets. Digging around in his travel belt pack he produced a bank card, and waving it at 'Ale, asked,

"Do you think they will take this?"

Still shocked, 'Ale asked the ticket agent if there were three seats available on the plane.

"Yes," she replied.

"How much they would cost?", 'Ale asked.

Once given the total amount, the little man said, "Yes, put it on my card."

He explained that he had been holding back some tithe money since earlier in the year waiting for God to show him where to invest it. When he heard that there were people, including a toddler, standing outside the airport on their way to reach out to Aboriginal people in his home nation, he knew it was God telling him to pay their tickets.

He carried within him God's heart for the indigenous people of his land. God had asked him to come on a short-term mission trip to Tonga. His team had just arrived in Tonga three days before, and was staying at the YWAM base. We had not met this man over the past three days, nor had we shared with anyone from his team about our financial needs.

"God brought me here to bless YOUR people, and you are going to do 'my' job in my home nation by reaching out to the Aboriginal people. I want to invest in that!", he declared.

After the remaining tickets were issued, we put the bags we had packed in faith the night before on the scales to check-in. We were really going, even though we went to the airport without tickets! All the airport personnel KNEW us, KNEW what we were doing, and KNEW we did not have tickets until God showed up! They had seen us for so many days prayer-walking to the airport in the early morning, with Fungani in a stroller. Now they saw us rejoicing, and they saw the simple man who paid for the tickets. Also, they saw us thank God. He acted SUDDENLY… Just as He said he would!

They announced that the plane was delayed, which was perfect for us so that we could actually stand and talk to our benefactor and get to know him. He handed us money to go get something to eat and drink while we waited, and we began to talk. His heart for the people of Australia was so obviously God's heart. His joy in giving to us was genuine. He told the story of overhearing the staff praying for people who were waiting at the airport without tickets, and of his conviction to go and give his tithe to the Lord by buying their tickets. He took a wad of money out of his belt pack and stuffed it into 'Ale's hand.

"What is this?" asked 'Ale with surprise.

"It is Australian money, and it is no good to me in Tonga," the gentle man answered. Then, as we continued to talk and share about our families and our lives, he again reached into his belt pack and jammed a wad of money into my hands with the same explanation. Again and again he did this, until 'Ale and I both had crumpled bills bulging out of pocket and purse. Finally, the call came to board, and we were so thankful for the extra hour and a half to get to know this lovely man!

As we entered the departure lounge, I quickly went into the ladies bathroom, the only "private" place to count the money from 'Ale's pockets and my purse. It totaled AU$1,900! Our friend had purchased tickets for us from Tonga to Sydney, Australia, but we needed to go on to Townsville, and those tickets could not be purchased at the airport where we started. That part of the trip was with a different airline whose personnel were not at the airport that day.

We decided to use this extra money to help buy our tickets from Sydney. We arrived in Sydney and had an overnight before going on to Townsville the next day. I began looking frantically for tickets online to Townsville. I found three seats open on a different flight than 'Ale, but still on the same day. Totaling up the cost, it was within pennies of the amount of money that our mystery friend had shoved into our hands! God knew! He orchestrated it all. It was a bunch of "suddenlies".

The man had also put a separate amount of money into 'Ale's hands, and told him to use it to purchase a video camera duty-free in the Sydney airport so that we could record the tour for him. That way he could share in what God was doing by watching it.

We took footage all during the four weeks we were gone. By the time the tour was over, the man had returned from his own outreach to Tonga and was back home near Sydney. We made arrangements to meet with him at a youth hostel downtown with a video room. We so enjoyed showing him videos of the tour of the faces of people he had helped bring to Jesus. He cried as he thanked God for allowing him to be part of reaching Aboriginal and Torres Strait islanders with the good news.

"I could never be as successful among them as you brown-skinned people have been," he told us.

What a privilege to be His hands and feet. What an honor to represent Him and His love for the people we met. What a privilege to be part of seeing over three hundred people make first-time commitments to follow Jesus. What an amazing God, who acted suddenly, though He knew all along how this faith journey would go. All those prayer walks to the airport were worth it!

Revelation

God is generous; He loves to give to his children.

He will provide all you need to fulfill your destiny.

You are a Son or a Daughter and your heavenly Father will provide for you.

You can live in a world of inheritance instead of the world of sowing and reaping.

Giving and obedience unlock the door of inheritance.

Application

Begin a lifestyle of giving.

If you tithe and give off the top you will always have enough.

Seek the Holy Spirit for a strategy to fulfill your vision.

Expand your vision and your provision will always follow.

Chapter 6: Setting the Captives Free
Kevin Stark

One of the things Team Xtreme feels they are called to do is to set the captives free. Through this mandate, we have seen open doors to go and preach the good news of freedom in Jesus to thousands of inmates in prisons in over forty nations around the world. Here are some of our favorite testimonies.

Holy Ghost Riot
One night, at a prison in California, the Holy Spirit showed up in an unusual way. We were having a time of preaching, teaching, and performing feats of strength, when suddenly the Holy Spirit began to fill the room. All over the room people began to weep, laugh, fall to the ground, and repent of their sins. This was during the early days of our ministry, and I did not have very much experience in visitations from the Holy Spirit. I had no clue what to do, so I grabbed one of the guys who could sing and told him to go sing something in the microphone. We were just a bunch of untrained, big strong guys who loved Jesus, so the only song that he could remember the words to was Amazing Grace.

He kept singing it over and over, and as he sang the power and presence of God increased. After a while, you could see all sorts of God-ordained activity around the room. People were lying on the floor here and there. They were getting deliverance from demons and being healed. This went on for some time until one of the guards came into our small room, and he told us that our time was up. The inmates needed to report back to their cells for lock down.

As the men began to leave the meeting room, they spilled out into the courtyard where hundreds of the prisoners were just hanging out. This is where the Holy Ghost riot began to happen. Randomly, one of the inmates began chanting, "Jesus, Jesus, Jesus." Soon, all of the inmates

44

who were still full of the Holy Spirit from the meeting joined in. Then, other inmates who did not attend the meeting joined in.

It sounded like we were at a huge youth conference, and the chant of a few men turned into a roar of hundreds. Men were pounding their fists into the air, and others had their hands lifted towards Heaven as the presence of God filled the whole prison. Men who were not at the meeting began to be touched by the power of God. It was as though Jesus Himself showed up, and an unannounced revival began to touch people. Keep in mind that we were in a state prison where this type of activity was not allowed. In fact, it was considered to be a riot situation. Soon, guards spilled out into the courtyard and commanded the chanting to stop. After a few more courses it died down, but as we walked out of the prison doors, still filled with the awe of God, we knew that we had just experienced a heavenly visitation.

Satanic Leader Saved

As our team entered a prison in the Midwest, we were warned by the Chaplain that there was a group of Satan-worshipers who might attend and disrupt our meeting. Our team got very excited because they are warriors, and they love a good fight. They knew that the battle had already been won by Jesus.

The meeting went really well. The team had a great altar call with many salvations, healings, and deliverances. However, after this victory the demons decided to make their move.

A man from the back of the room came forward and began to mock what was going on. Some unproductive arguing went on for a while, and then one of the inmate Christians asked if we could prove to him that Jesus is real. We took the man into another room, and we began to pray and worship. There were several inmate Christians and our team members who began to pray in the Spirit, and began to cast out the demon that had the man in bondage.

45

The man began to manifest and went into convulsions. All of a sudden, the power of God hit him, and he literally left the ground and flew back and slammed against the wall. Our team and the local Christians began to pray over him on the ground, and demons began to leave his body. Every time a demon left more peace and power came in. By the time we had left, all the demons were gone. He prayed to follow Jesus and was baptized in the Holy Spirit, and he began worshiping God.

We found out later that he was the leader of the Satanic church in the prison. His assignment from hell was to go to different states and commit a crime so he would get thrown in jail. From there he would start a Satanic church and make disciples while serving his time, assign leaders, and move on to another state to repeat the process. Just like the demon-possessed Gergesenes in the Bible, this man was totally set free. I am sure that he went on to plant Christian churches instead of satanic ones.

Washed in the Blood
Often we have intercessors travel with us as we do our ministry. The International House of Prayer has become great friends and partners as we walk together to see the glory of the Lord cover the earth. One of our intercessors, Mama Bev from IHOP, was with us in a prison. We began to minister to the inmates that had come forward. She had the opportunity to pray with a young man that needed to be set free.

He had murdered a man. Even though he had given his life to Jesus since then, he could not get the thoughts of the crime out of his mind. Every time he would look at his hands, he would see the blood of the man on his hands, and the shame and guilt would almost drive him insane. Momma Bev and the Holy Spirit went to work. Together they walked through some steps of deliverance. She prayed the blood of Jesus over him and broke the curse. When he opened his eyes and looked at his hands, for the first time since the murder, there was no blood. His hands had been washed white as snow!

Nothing is impossible with God, and nobody is unreachable or too far gone to be saved. The blood of Jesus is all-powerful to save, heal, and deliver the lost. This is how the captives are getting set free.

Forgiven
Often the living conditions in the prisons in third world countries that we visit are horrible. Several men are usually housed together in a small 10' x 10' rat-infested cell, with dirt floors, and a bucket in the corner of the room for a toilet. Diets typically consist only of bread, rice, and water. Because of the living conditions in such places, violence and rage manifest frequently. Men who are put into prison for any crime are locked up with murderers and rapists, which only promotes more violence and more murders.

The Brazilian prisons are known to be some of the worst in the world. When our team was in a prison in Fortaleza, we were in what I would call the pit of all pits. This pit was full of some of worst criminals in Brazil. As we began our program you could feel the spiritual battle going on in the atmosphere of the room. But as we prayed and preached, the cloud was lifting and the light was overcoming the darkness. The dimly light room that was packed with men with hearts of stone was soon filled with men laughing, cheering, and being touched by God.

When we gave the alter call, most of the men responded to the call of forgiveness. We began to minister the love of the Father to the fatherless, and tears began to fall. One of the last men who came forward had a question about the mercy of God.

He asked, "Can God forgive anything?"

I answered, "Yes."

He asked again, "Can He forgive someone who has killed 5 men?"

I said, "Yes, He can."

We prayed together. I ministered the love of God to him, and we hugged. It is amazing how simply and quickly someone can be saved! Many of the men started the day in the pit and ended up in God's penthouse in a few minutes!

Revelation

The father loves those in prison.

As you serve those in prison it is like you are doing it to Jesus.

No sin under the sun is beyond being forgiven.

Part of every person's ministry is to serve the least, the lost, and the last.

People in prison are behind physical bars, but there are many people who are free in the world, but imprisoned in their hearts and behind spiritual bars.

Application

Start to read books on deliverance.

If you have any addictions or bondages in your life, set a path for freedom.

Be part of a church that teaches and walks in deliverance.

Make deliverance and freedom a part of your ministry.

Chapter 7: Welcome To My World: Aotearoa
Jason Hotere

The Pre-Tour Phase
The first person to get things rolling for my part in preparing for a full
Team Xtreme tour in New Zealand was a man named Marty Emmett.
He took us to Opunake, New Zealand—the more commonly known
name of the Maori's Aotearoa—to meet Pastor Murray McEwen and
to speak at a fundraiser. Opunake is a small town of about 1,500
people in the Taranaki Region of the North Island of New Zealand.
The goal was to try to raise the $8,000 needed to bring in one team to
their region, but if that goal was not met, the team would not be
invited.

Rick (my partner) and I performed a few strength feats, and shared
about our experiences. Marty got up to share, and everyone was
excited.

All he said was, "So, how much do you want to give? These guys
have shared it all."

The Community Center was a beehive of activity, and the activity was
not wasted. After the desserts were served, and the contributions were
counted, the total amount collected came to $12,000! The place
erupted into cheers, but even with that announcement some cynics did
not believe it. We knew that only God could have moved on people's
hearts, and it was the first of many times we would see God move in
New Zealand.

After that first show in Opunake, we did a Church Based Outreach in
a few schools in Marty's home city of Wanganui. When it was time
for the evening performance, Rick had to fly home because his wife
had a serious illness. This was the first time I did the whole show by
myself, but God moved again. It is easy when it is just you and Jesus.

Marty also took us to Hastings and Napier on the other side of the
North Island, in Hawke's Bay. We also traveled to Dannevirke in the

lower central part of the North Island, but Dannevirke really stands out as a memorable experience.

We met with Pastor Mark of Dannevirke to check out the church building for the performance.

The helpers from the church put out all the chairs and said to me, "Well, that is all the chairs we have." (I believe there were 300 to 350 chairs set up.)

I asked, "Is there any way we can get more people in?"

They said, "If we have to, we can open up the cafe hall."

I said in faith, "We may have to do that!"

That night, the hall was so packed that not only was the cafe hall opened up, but they had to leave the outside doors open too. It was actually a fire hazard, and because there were people too close to the stage, we had to take one of our favorite strength feats involving fire off our list. It was just too crowded.

It was an amazing evening, though. When we gave the altar call, people had to stay where they were, and we got everyone to pray in their seats.

Pastor Mark was surprised and said, "If this is the result of just you two performers, I need to get some help for when the three teams come!"

We performed pre-shows in cities up and down the lengths of both the North and South Islands, including Wellington, Christchurch, Dunedin, all the way down south to Invercargill, back up to Nelson and Blenheim, and up toward Auckland in Hamilton on the North Island again.

When in Hamilton, the Coordinator, Michael Low, had us come to an Anglican church for the youth there. We heard that the parents were also coming, and that they had said they would take their children out of the program if they thought it was an inappropriate message. It was understandable for them to be protective, but I knew God was going to show up.

This is my expectation every time I perform. Even when I am not on the stage, I talk to people, and I preach wherever I am. God wants to use me and you. All we have to do is to be willing.

It was like there was an explosion that night at the performance, and we had so much fun. When we gave the altar call for repentance and recommitment to Jesus, almost all the youth stood up. What was even more shocking was that the parents came forward with them!

We asked if anyone needed prayer for his or her health, and a young teenager put his hand up. He said he had been playing rugby and was injured badly enough to need a neck brace. Everyone there at the program knew what had happened to him. Even though the brace had been taken off, there was a bruise that still had not gone away. The bruise was so big that it was more like a bulge. We took him back stage and prayed for him. Within minutes the bulge had completely disappeared! I encouraged him to tell everyone what God had done.

The Full Shows
Everyone had finally arrived in Aotearoa including my team leader and team members, and all the other teams. It was like family times again. Everyone I knew in my country was able to actually meet the people they had heard so much about in my seven years of travel all over the world with Team Xtreme. These were the fellows who were there during my personal battles, including even oppression from the devil. These guys were now with me in my country along with the family members I had been praying for over many years.

Before the full tour, we had a commissioning night at the City Elim Church in Auckland Central. The place was packed with celebrities, pastors, dignitaries, business people, church-goers, and most importantly, the teams. My face was beaming from ear-to-ear. We were ready to rock Aotearoa!

We met at the Auckland YWAM Base the next day for the drive to our first city. It was the city of Gisbourne, the city that is said to get the first rays of sunshine every day in the Western world.

I was asked if I would drive the truck and trailer. I was quite worried about the load as I knew there was a bridge on the way, and the load might be too high to go under it. I had already had some of the fellows go ahead so they could call me and give me the height of the bridge before we got there. We started off with three large buses, trailers, and vans filled with support teams, along with private cars and the truck I drove with the skate ramps. We were headed for a five to six-hour drive to the southeast part of the North Island, to an area called the Poverty Bay region.

I received the phone call about the bridge height after stopping only an hour out from Auckland. My load had shifted, and I had to pull into a lumberyard to use their fork lift and maneuver the load around to make it safe. I was told that the bridge was way too low for the load to go under, so I decided to stop in Tauranga and wait. I left the truck there and got a ride with one of my team drivers to Gisbourne. Tatiana, and a friend from GX (Global eXpression), Tamie, drove our car ahead of me and were waiting for me to arrive. It was almost midnight when I finally got there. We were going to have to start the show without the skate ramps.

Gisbourne, January 21st, 2004
Impact World Tour New Zealand was underway in Gisbourne, and right away I had an opportunity to trust God to move. This show was to be the first time that I would attempt to flip a car over onto its roof. The car we were using was a Honda Accord, and was pretty heavy when I practiced trying to lift it. I could not lift it in the practice, but I expected that the adrenaline from the excitement of the show and the crowd would propel me to accomplish this strongman feat.

Minutes before the start, Kevin Stark added to the excitement of the moment when he came to me and said, "Jay, you are preaching tonight. This is your time. This is the day you have been waiting for."

As if I needed any more pressure, the looming clouds also pointed to the inevitability of rain.

As the opening video played, the crowd was silent. Then an eruption of excitement came from the people as our team members poured onto the stage. Screams and whistles filled the Awapuni Stadium as Rick, our emcee for the evening, yelled out, "Make some n-o-i-s-e!"

The team members blew up hot water bottles, bent steel bars in their teeth and on their heads, lifted a 150kg log overhead, had a human tug-of-war, and broke stacks of concrete. Each feat of strength was designed to depict a parable of the struggle everyone goes through every day—the struggle between right and wrong, the struggle between heaven and hell. This represented the spiritual battle going on over our lives to show what Jesus has done for us, so that we can be born again and have a new life.

The rain eventually poured down, and it seemed like everyone started to go home. What could we do?

When the crowd left, we thought they were going to get out of the rain. In fact, they were just going to their cars to grab anything that would protect them from the rain—raincoats, blankets, tarpaulins, and even plastic rubbish bags with holes cut out for the head. Only in New Zealand! What an amazing sight!

I came out on stage, and the rain was falling. I told the crowd about my life, and it felt like everyone knew exactly what I was talking about. Many of them probably did.

As I slowly worked my way down to the grassy area from the stage toward the car, I said, "Picture yourself in the passenger seat of this car, and someone is in total control of where you are going, but you have no say in it."

This was actually a depiction of my life. Before I knew Jesus I was heading into a place of depression, hatred, and anger towards life. I even contemplated suicide. With how I felt, I didn't know what else I could do but kill myself. These were the things I was sharing with the crowd.

I ended by saying, "Don't let the devil control your destiny. All he wants to do is to steal, kill and destroy you, and if he is in control that is what he will do."

At that point I bent down to flip the car over. I knew it would not be easy because of the rain, but the car did eventually turn over.

I finished by saying, "God will flip your world upside down. He will do it not to destroy you, but to get your attention so you know He is in control. He will do it because He knows our lives need a change."

Hundreds came to the front of the stage--children, mothers, fathers, and even whole families. I remembered the words Jesus spoke while He was on the earth, "Even a prophet is not honored in his own town."

I remembered also the words the Lord spoke when I first landed in New Zealand from the U.S.A.

"Because of My death and resurrection, Jason, you will do more and greater things than I did."

Even though it was my "hometown", Jesus still moved powerfully. I felt relieved when the first show was over, and now we could proceed to shake the rest of Aotearoa!

Dangers of Performing with Team Xtreme
There are many stories worth remembering from this tour, but not all of them were positive. There are real dangers when you are a member of Team Xtreme—some physical and some spiritual. One of the spiritual dangers was illustrated when one of the local leaders got very angry after our show when I had finished preaching. His concern was how I gave the altar call. It was not how he felt it should have been done, and he wasn't used to the way I did it.

I had shared from my heart, and had made the altar call the way I felt the Lord was leading me, but there is room for differences of opinion. It wasn't the difference in viewpoints that was so harmful, however. Despite the many hundreds that came forward that night, he shouted and screamed at me, and the female assistant coordinator of the city. She was actually brought to tears because of his shouting at her.

My friend, Drew Fitzpatrick, was there trying to defuse the situation. He was trying to help the leader focus on the positive by pointing out how many people had come forward. I apologized to the now tearful young coordinator for the verbal abuse she had received. It didn't personally upset me that much, but it still was a reminder that we don't always get praised for doing what we believe the Lord Jesus wants us to do.

Another kind of spiritual danger came out at the show in Tauranga, Bay of Plenty. I was scheduled to pull a semi-rig across the field in front of the crowd even though that night was rainy. We always try to make safety our first concern, but we all forgot that night to let the driver know that they were to take their foot off the brakes, including the air brakes, when I dropped my arm. That truck did not go anywhere. We could easily have become very upset with each other and given into the enemy's desire to sow disunity among the team. It was one more lesson in learning to make sure everyone is on the same page and to clearly communicate to avoid misunderstandings.

The other type of danger is physical. The following occurred up at our show in Tokoroa, Central North Island. An American, named Nathan Buskamp, was to run through three sets of burning 2x4's that were fourteen feet long. The three sets of boards would be held by six men chest high as Nathan ran towards them.

We lit the three sets of 2x4's, and Nathan ran as fast as he could, hitting the first set with his chest. As he broke through, he slipped and started to fall towards the second set of 2x4's. He hit the second set with his head, right on the part of the wood that was on fire. He let out a yell, but he continued running through the remaining two sets of boards. He broke through with complete disregard for his injury as he lifted his arms in triumph. While the crowd was yelling wildly, everyone behind the stage was looking for the paramedics! Nathan just wanted to get back on stage because he had a brick break next, and he was to jump off from a seven-foot high scaffold into a set of bricks. As his leader, I stepped in and held him back from possible further injury because safety is first in our shows.

Wellington, February 19, 2004 (*needs bullet-point)
Whatever the danger, whether spiritual or physical, trusting in the Lord through prayer is the way through. The show in New Zealand's capital city, Wellington, showed the truth of that.

The weather forecast was for thunderstorms, hail, and even hurricane force winds, but Team Xtreme was set to perform. I was waiting for the words, "No show." David Cole and Mark Anderson gave the go-ahead, so we were going ahead with the show in four hours. We started setting up for the show, and right after that was done we started praying.

It was the first time I would perform on a stage with rain blowing sideways— actually almost parallel to the ground! The wind was screaming through the sides of the stage, and we could not see the crowd because of the downpour and the lights glaring at us from the reflection of the rain.

To be honest, I was concerned, but I went ahead and screamed, "Let's rock the house!"

We had people praying, but there was hardly a let up with the weather.

Kevin gave me the microphone, and said, "Preach your heart out."

I walked to the front of the stage and started to preach. Five minutes later, I could not see the crowd, so I stood there and began praying into the microphone.

"Jesus, can you stop the rain so I could talk about you?"

No more than two to three minutes later the rain slowed down. When I was ready to give the altar call, I looked up and saw a patch of blue sky surrounded by darkness.

I looked at the crowd again, and said, "This is the power of Jesus when you pray to Him. He hears and answers. Thank you Jesus!"

Even though there were many fewer there that night than usual—about 1,200 brave people—it broke something in the spirit realm. Darkness can never prevail where there is light. I found out later that, while everyone was in the stadium praying for the rain to stop, there was also a youth group from a church also praying. They had walked around the stadium in prayer seven times, and the end of the seventh time around the rain stopped! Prayer is powerful.

A National Audience
One-third of the population of New Zealand is in Auckland. Kevin Stark and I were asked to share on a national prime-time program that reached almost 500,000 people nightly, called, "The Paul Holmes Show." Since Kevin isn't from around there, he thought it was called the "Paul *Homes* Show".

He actually said, "Wow, this is a first for me going on a home and garden show."

I laughed, but then explained that this guy pretty much could lift you up, or rip you apart. He had used his show sometimes in ways hostile to Christians, and had even made fools out of one particular Christian organization.

I was prepared for battle, and told Kevin, "The moment this guy rips into us about Jesus, I am letting him have it with all guns blazing!"

Kevin saw that I needed prayer. All the way up to Auckland from Hamilton we prayed that God would not be put down, and that we would exalt His name while still honoring Mr. Holmes.

When we met Paul he was quite pleasant. That made a lot of sense, of course, since Kevin and I are both six feet tall and had with us steel bars, a baseball bat, a stack of bricks, and phonebooks to rip. Not many guys would look to pick a fight!

I set everything up while Kevin was talking to Mr. Holmes behind his desk. Then the program started. I began by bending the steel bars in my teeth, and Kevin broke a bat. Then we broke to a story. As we began to talk, Mr. Holmes asked what the significance of what I had just done was.

I told him, "Everything we did had a story to it. Just like Jesus used parables to get His message across, so do we."

He then asked specifically about the phonebooks, and Kevin said to me, "Here's your chance to preach to your nation."

At that moment, I declined, and asked Kevin to share the story.

The time for the final feat of the show came—the brick-break.

Right before I was to perform, Mr. Holmes asked again, "What is the significance of this feat of strength?"

This time, I was ready.

I replied, "There is a separation between man and God. This wall of bricks represents sin. Sin includes our selfishness, anger, sexual immorality, adultery, pornography, and other things. That separation is broken when people realize they are heading on a downward spiral and need help. That was the way my life was going. I wanted to commit suicide, and there was no way I could see how my life could change. I cried out to Jesus and said, 'Jesus if you are real, show me or I am out of here!'

I gave my life and heart to Jesus on the 26th of November, 1989, at 4:45 p.m. Mr. Holmes, my wall was broken, and my sin was broken with it."

We broke the bricks. Then to my surprise, Mr. Holmes said to me, "Yep, share that."

Kevin said to me, "Now it is your turn to preach to your nation!"

What a privilege to tell over half-a-million New Zealanders that Jesus lives, and that He wants to rescue them from a life of hopelessness. Months and even years after I spoke, people still remember that time. Most importantly, Jesus was talked about on national television. Thank you, Lord!

Many who see our shows have never witnessed a presentation of the gospel the way Team Xtreme presents it. We need to get into the communities to share more. Sometimes, ministries will focus on building up numbers or programs, but the one who has called and sent all of us is the one and only Jesus Christ, the Lord and Savior. We preach Jesus. He is the message, not our team or our ministry. He brings the conviction. That is the only way people receive salvation and new life, through Jesus Christ. We need to repent, for the Kingdom of God draws near.

Revelation

God has a heart for the nations, but he also has a heart for your family

God shines brightest in the darkest places.

God opens doors that no man can open, and shuts doors no man can shut.

Miracles happen when you speak out what God spoke to you first in the secret place.

Application

Trust God for your nation. Pray every day for a historical revival to come to your family, city, region, and nation.

Begin to write down and speak out the desires of your heart.

Share your promises and vision from God every day with someone. At least once a week, speak out loud your vision for your nation.

Take one hour to pray and write down your goals for the next year, 5 years, and 10 years. Focus on 5 areas—spiritual, family, financial, mental, and physical.

Chapter 8: To the Jew First
Kevin Stark

One of the mandates the Lord has given Team Xtreme is to take the good news of Jesus Christ to the Jews first. Because of this mandate, we take teams each year to Israel to preach the gospel to the Jews. The Lord has opened up doors in amazing ways over the years, and we have seen many Jews come to follow Yeshua as their Savior.

Since we started carrying out our assignment to the Jewish people, God has begun to change the way we think about His chosen people and their role in the Kingdom of God. The following are some of the revelations that He has given us over the years.

The Abrahamic Covenant that was given to the Jews is an eternal covenant that is not affected by the New Covenant, and it still applies to every Jew today.

The Jewish people are God's chosen people, and they are still leading His plan for the Kingdom of God—past, present, and future.

The Promised Land, which includes Jerusalem, still belongs to God and He has given it to the Jews.

The role of the Gentiles is to provoke the Jews to jealousy through their love, prayer, and Holy Spirit power to cause them to seek after Yeshua.

God has a call for one new man as written about by the Apostle Paul in Ephesians 2:15. We are becoming more sensitive to this question: are the Jewish man and the Gentile man coming together in spirit and truth to form the one new man in Jesus?

Our calling to come to the land of Israel was given to me one day while I was in the Global Prayer Room at International House of Prayer. I heard the Lord say, "Return to My land and preach the gospel." I had already been to Israel about 30 years before where I met my beautiful wife-to-be, Laura. Israel had already clearly blessed me, and now God was calling me to bless it in return.

After 30 years away from "the promised land" we were going back with a new assignment—to show the Jewish people the Kingdom of God and to love them back into it. Our passion and understanding about Yeshua, and a demonstration of His power, were to be a part of God's plan in calling His people home. The forming of the one new man is the process of redeeming man back to his original design. It includes the Gentile man's receiving revelation of the Jewish roots of the church, and the Jewish man's receiving revelation that Yeshua is the Messiah. In the process of walking out the redemption, and growing in that revelation of the cross, one new man begins to be formed.

One of my favorite stories about this process of forming the one new man happened in the Negev (the southern part of Israel) in 2006. It was just after the "Road to Peace" agreement had given the Gaza strip back to the Palestinians. Thousands of Jews were quickly removed from the West Bank, losing everything in the move. A lot of displaced Jews had been relocated to the Negev deserts in trailers, and were waiting for plans to build a new city. After a day of wonderful fellowship with these Jews, many of whom were Orthodox, we were taken to the place they were going to build their synagogue. They began to share their dreams of their new city in great detail and with passion. Like many centuries before, when the Jews had been rejected, their belongings were taken from them, and they were beaten down and even killed. But once again they were showing resiliency that can only come from God.

As we concluded our time together, my wife asked the Jewish leaders if we could pray together. Our friend who had brought us to the meeting tried to explain that Jews and Gentiles do not pray together, trying to provide a way for us to get out of an awkward situation. However, God has a plan for one new man that is much greater than our thoughts and understanding.

One of the Jewish leaders spoke up while looking at my wife, and said, "You know, sometimes the older brother will put his younger sister on top of his shoulders so they can see father together."

He then extended an invitation for her to pray. My wife started to pray fervently, and the spirit of God fell on everyone there. Next, the Orthodox priest prayed the rabbi's blessing over all of us, and there was another wave of the Spirit that hit us. I believe something was birthed in the heavens that day, and Father was pleased. What a wonderful day.

Since we have been going back to Israel on an annual basis, we have seen the number of Messianic Jews there increasing every year. Every trip we take we see more Jews coming to faith in Yeshua, being healed, and being delivered.

As I walk out a continuing revelation of God's heart for the Jews, I have come to several conclusions. The first conclusion is that God does not love the Jews more than the other nations of the world. However, He did make an everlasting covenant with the Jews, and He does have a specific plan and purpose for this chosen people which has yet to be fulfilled. God could have chosen any nation, but he chose the Jews to fulfill this part of His plan.

In John 3:16, it says for God so loved *THE WORLD,* that he gave his only son, that whoever believed in Him would not perish but will have everlasting life. God's love, salvation, and living the Kingdom life is for every nation in the world. The gospel and the love of God will continue to go out to every person, nation, and generation, until the Great Commission is complete.

Revelation

I believe that replacement theology, the belief that the Christian church is the new Israel—a belief that is prevalent in our churches today—is in reality a false doctrine. I believe we should seek the Lord

63

for his wisdom and understanding for both the Jew and the Gentile in these end days.

As you bless the Jewish people, you will also be blessed by our Father in Heaven (Genesis 12:3).

There is a great plan for both the Jew and the Gentile in the Kingdom of God.

Application

Pray for the Jews and Israel.

Look for ways to bless Israel and their people.

Take a trip to Israel. It will change your life.

Keep loving and preaching the gospel to both the Jews and Gentiles.

Incorporate the Jewish festivals into your church for greater understanding and revelation.

Chapter 9: Real Warriors Pray
Kevin Stark

For a good portion of my Christian life, I wasn't that much into intercession (praying for souls). I thought prayer was for little old ladies with blue bee-hive hairdos. It seemed like nearly every intercessor I knew in the early days of my ministry had a weird "do"!

With my idea of what an intercessor looked like, I could spot them a long way off. Of course, most of them were very nice, and I knew in theory at least they were very necessary. I just thought they were a bit strange.

As an evangelist, though, I wanted them to be a part of my team. My team was all about soul-winning, and everybody knew that a real soul-winner had an intercessor or two as part of his team. I didn't want to get beat up by the devil when I was out preaching, so I recruited a few to pray for us while we were on the road. Needless to say, my prayer life at this time was very dull and shallow.

The problem of my dull prayer life was obviously due to my own set of wrong thoughts about prayer. I thought of myself as a warrior, and I believed warriors needed to be where the action was—one mile from the gates of hell, pulling people out of the pit just before they were destroyed.

I knew I should be praying, and I did pray some. My short prayers were sent up usually in between what I thought were the real battles, and were prayed mostly for the wrong reasons. I thought the real battle for men of God was not to be fought while shut inside a prayer room, but out on the battlefield. Little did I know that the Lord was about to change all that by leading me to the International House of Prayer in Kansas City (IHOPKC).

My first visit to the IHOPKC Global Prayer Room was back in 1999. I was not that impressed. The building was an old double-wide trailer with ugly carpet and a few musicians singing. Every few minutes, a fellow would pray, the musicians would repeat part of the prayer in song, and they would do that over and over. The repetition really bugged me at first because I was in a judgmental mindset. I've since learned that you cannot receive from anything or anyone you are judging.

In spite of my negative outlook from my first visit, I went back, and the next few times I found myself starting to enjoy it. Up until then, I thought prayer was a thing to be endured, but something else was being birthed in me. I was not sure what it was yet, but it felt good, and I was actually beginning to enjoy prayer.

Another positive was that I noticed, on the bulletin board right outside of the prayer room, were pictures of our ministry from the Impact World Tour. If these guys were praying for us they had to be ok!

Still, something that troubled me about IHOPKC was some of their language in prayer. It just did not fit into my world. Phrases like "love sick", "the Bride of Christ", "eat the scroll"—it all sounded a bit feminine to me. You have to understand that the guys on our team were convicts, gang members, rednecks, athletes, and other hard-core types who were survivors of life. For us to express ourselves in ways that seemed soft, emotional, or weak was not acceptable to us at the time. We thought God was tough, and we were called to destroy as many works of the devil as we could during our lifetimes.

In spite of all these negative reactions, I continued to go to the Global Prayer Room (GPR). I even started to realize that I was becoming a bit addicted to my time there. It was like needing a fix, and I wanted to be there every day. Even on my busiest days, if I could just sneak over to the prayer room for 15 minutes it would satisfy my soul. My heart began to soften, and my mind was changing in its understanding about the purpose of prayer. I was falling in love with Jesus all over again, and the Prayer Room was where we would meet.

It seemed to the fellows on our team, who weighed 300 pounds with tattoos showing, and who had muscles bulging from the day's workout, that they did not really fit into the prayer room culture of skinny jeans and flannel shirts. Once the team members got past the surface of things though, their hearts also began to soften just like mine had. Another positive was that, as I continued to visit there, I began to see many of the leaders of YWAM around the world— whom I consider to be like apostles on steroids—come to the GPR river to be refreshed and restored to the place of their original design. To be worshipers and lovers first before becoming workers.

I also found out that Mike Bickle, the head coach of the GPR, came from a background similar to mine. He was a sports star in school, his dad was a champion boxer, and he grew up being what the world calls a "man's man". Even though we didn't talk much, we would playfully slug each other or deliver a quick forearm blast while passing by— which, in a man's world, means "I like you". I don't think there were many other guys he could slug in the GPR!

As I listened to a lot of Mike's teaching, it began to resonate in my soul as truth even though there were a lot of new thoughts and words. New revelations from Heaven began to change the way I thought, and this changed the way I acted, and eventually it changed the way I lived. I would often be walking in the prayer room when I would hear the Lord's voice simply say, "Kevin, I love you" over and over.

As you read this on paper, it probably does not do much to strike you, but when you hear the voice of God speaking that over you, it messes you up! This drew me to a level of worship and intimacy I had never known before. I would be taken into heavenly places and lose all track of time and space. I just wanted to be with Jesus. I discovered how much I needed to be in the presence of God to be effective in partnering with Him for His Kingdom as an evangelist and a forerunner to the nations. The time in the GPR for our team was so life-changing that it wasn't too long before we began to implement the IHOPKC model of prayer and worship when Team Xtreme was on the road.

During the Impact World Tour to New Zealand, we had a grueling schedule which included multiple cities all over the country with 300 events all in a period of 90 days. Many times we had five to six evening shows a week (not counting school assemblies in the mornings). Yet every afternoon we would soak with the IHOPKC style of worship, and we would pray for our evening event. As a result of our prayer times, our team stayed spiritually and physically strong. No one got sick, and everyone was fired up and ready to go each day, even with all the events. Back at home in Kansas City, IHOPKC had made a commitment to Impact World Tour to pray for us 24 hours a day, 7 days a week, for the entire 90 days of the New Zealand tour.

The impact of this tour was amazing. We shared the gospel with hundreds of thousands, and saw 65,000 make Jesus Christ the Lord of their lives. This tour included wonderful testimonies, healings, signs and wonders on earth and in the heavens, financial provision, and much, much more.

One of our many highlights of partnership with IHOPKC was the Student Awakening, which started November 9, 2009, and continued until the following October of 2010. While I was on the road in Spain and Morocco I heard about the Awakening services. I heard that students were repenting of sin, many people were getting physical healing, and hundreds were coming to Christ and being water baptized. I had just returned from the Spanish and Moroccan outreach, and was totally wiped out from intense spiritual warfare, traveling, and uncomfortable living conditions. I went straight from the airport to the Awakening service, and could hardly believe the presence of God I felt when I walked in.

The atmosphere felt electrified with the joy of the Lord. At first, I just stood around and observed what was going on, but then I soon jumped into the river. It was like Heaven had come down to earth! I was immediately filled with joy, love, and peace, and my fatigued body felt totally energized. I had been to many awakenings around the world, but I had never felt or seen anything like this.

The partnership between Team Xtreme and IHOPKC over the past 14 years has been an amazing one. My time in the GPR has completely changed my family, our team, and me. At the beginning of this journey of intimacy, I thought prayer was all about my ministry, and about me, but as I traveled the road I discovered the GPR was all about Him. Even so, He still says it is all about me because He loves me so much. I hope you can follow that logic. I will probably never become a full-time intercessory missionary, but I have become a worshiping warrior, helping to prepare the way for the return of my First Love.

Thanks to my heroes in the faith: Mike Bickle, Lou Engle, Wes Hall, Cory Russell, Allen Hood, and all the worship teams of IHOPKC. Together we are pressing on for a third Great Awakening, and the Second Coming of our King Jesus.

Revelation

The purpose of my life is to worship.

Time equals intimacy. You will give your time, talent, and treasures to whatever or whomever you love.

Revelation is a process that brings you to the place of your original design and purpose.

Worship and prayer work best together.

Application

Attend a conference on the subject of growing in intimacy with God through prayer and worship.

Visit and commit to a house of prayer in your area, or start a prayer room in your home.

Commit to at least one hour of prayer and worship each day.

Chapter 10: Fighting a New Fight
Manor Kumar Chopra

I was born and brought up in Raipur, the capital city of the new state of Chhattisgarh, in a staunch Hindu family. Chhattisgarh used to be a part of the State of Madhya Pradesh, and is in the east central part of the country.

I grew up to be a tall and physically strong man. I considered that to be my biggest asset, and I used it to show my power over everyone. I had a very short temper to go with my strength, and I could react quickly with my fist if anyone antagonized me. I got into many fights without much thought of the consequences. I didn't know why, but I realized that as I grew physically, I grew in anger and frustration too.

My fights left a trail of unhappy people around me. My parents even feared that one day I might kill someone. The only reason I was able to avoid jail was that my family was well known and respected. In order to escape the hatred I had caused in my native place, I moved to Bangalore. It was there I met Ragini, fell in love with her, and married her in 1990.

Living in a different place and having a wife did not solve my problems as I had hoped. I had the same pattern of bouts of anger and violent assaults on people who bothered me. I tried different businesses but did not have much success. I started a travel agency, and even tried real estate, but some friends cheated me and I lost all my money. After that, I just associated with different kinds of people who wanted to use me for my physique, kind of like a bodyguard. They took me to bars and hotels with them for protection, and sometimes I was hired as a bouncer as well. I really wasn't paying any attention to how I was living. I would simply get into fights and then into trouble.

This kind of lifestyle finally caught up with me. In one fight, in 1996, I hit a man in anger. I knocked some of his teeth out, and he was down on the ground for five minutes. I actually gave him some water

70

and took him to the hospital, but his family filed a police case against me, and I landed in jail. That shook me to the core. I could not believe that someone would dare do that to me.

I was ashamed of the bad image it would bring to my family. My relatives were telephoning about it. My daughter, who was just 5-years old at the time, asked my wife about me, but she could not bear to tell the child about the place I was in.

All this made me feel very small inside. The atmosphere in the jail was very bad with some 200 inmates crowded in a place meant for only 20 people. There was no proper toilet either, adding to the misery. I just sat in a corner for the 21 hours I was there, but the 21 hours seemed like 21 years to me, with each second seeming like a day.

During that time in jail I went through so much pain. I was very angry with the one whom I thought caused me to be in jail, and I kept thinking that when I got out I would take revenge on him. As I sat there in the cell, I noticed all of the pictures of different gods drawn on the walls.

In my desperation, I started praying to all the gods, saying, "If you help me get out I will visit 666 temples."

My only interest in gods and temples, up to that time, had been to keep a tradition of going to the native temple in my hometown of Dongargarh, 80 miles from our home. Going to this temple involved climbing 1,200 steps up the mountain where the temple was. When I was a child, I had done it mostly to please my parents and to enjoy the coconut we broke there. But as an adult, I had watched a TV documentary about some gods and started to learn more about them. In the difficult situation I was in, I remembered all that and thought maybe I should seek their help to get out of the mess I was in.

Just as I was thinking about all of this, a pastor I had known visited me in the jail. I was already so angry that I did not want to see him at all. Besides, I had never liked the Christians who always were trying to convince us to worship their God. My wife was interested in Christianity though, and had spoken to me many times about going to church.

When this pastor gave me a Bible and told me about the love of Jesus, I asked him, "Why are you talking to me? I am a Hindu. You had better leave this place right away if you know what is good for you!"

The pastor turned and left without another word, and shortly after that I got out. I had been in for 21 hours. My wife had managed to get the help of lawyers and a friend in government service to act as my guarantee, and they let me out on bail. I was greatly relieved to be out of that horrible place.

Even though I was out of jail, my problems were not over. The case against me still had to be faced. Besides this latest one, I had 10 more police cases against me from earlier fights. Because this last man I hit had pressed charges, my name was in the papers, and my shame was made public.

My family was put to shame, and they were all very unhappy with me. I was forced to face the reality of my choices of life and how it affected my wife, daughter, parents, and all of my other relatives. While I was in this stressed state of mind from having let down my entire family, I saw another pastor I knew approaching our house about a week after I got out of jail. I had met him many times in the gym where I worked out and had become friends with him.

Still frustrated with everyone, I thought, "If this man says one word about Jesus, I will beat him up!"

To my surprise he did not even mention the name of Jesus. He told me about some international champions that were visiting India (Team Xtreme). He said that they were planning to have a strength competition show and asked if I would be interested in going with him. I was excited to go, and was amazed at what I saw.

These men did such interesting feats of strength! When the pastor wanted to introduce me to them, I was thrilled. Since I admired what they did, and was keen on learning how to do these feats, I asked Kevin Stark and others on the team how they did these things. All of them had a similar answer. They said they prayed to the Lord Jesus, and it was He who gave them this ability. When I heard that, I felt anger rise up in me so strongly that I wanted to beat them all up, but I didn't even try. I thought they could be stronger than I was.

I snapped at the pastor, and said, "Will you take me home now, or should I walk?"

He did not argue and took me home.

That night I was frustrated and confused. I felt sad and could not sleep. I thought, "Everywhere I go people are talking about this Jesus!"

Suddenly, I didn't know what came over me. For the first time in my life I felt afraid of being alone. No one was speaking to me. My entire family was so sad because of my failures. My mother and father were crying about me and worried about my future. At that point, again for the first time in my life, I decided to pray to Jesus.

Kneeling, I said to Him, "I don't know who You are, but wherever I go people speak about you. If you really are God, give me these three things: forgiveness for all the wrongs that I have committed, admiration and love from people instead of the hate they have for me now, and the ability to be a strongman. Please give me power to do feats of strength and to become a champion."

I prayed for this for the next six months, and I made progress as a strongman. I was fully convinced that my achievements were because of my prayer to Jesus. Some of my friends had become aware I was praying every night for these things, and they knew that I was doing strength training at home. One night, I was praying about the second request I had made to Jesus, that people would like and admire me. The very next day, I got a call from a friend working in the Catholic school nearby asking me to be the guest for a function at the school and to talk to the older children there.

I was surprised at the invitation to such a big school of 2,000 students. I planned to entertain them with some of my feats. I knew that if they would looked at me as a hero I would be able to influence them with my words. I broke a brick, bent some steel, and ripped a big book. Since they were so young, I did that with some dramatization, and it kept their attention until the end of the demonstrations.

Afterward, I spoke briefly and said, "Jesus loves you."

They were all very much interested in what I did, and they did admire me! They wanted to talk to me after the show, and asked for my autograph. Some even wanted to touch me. This made me feel good after all the shame I had to face after being in jail. I knew it was one of the three things I had asked God to give me, and I was very happy about beginning to see the answer.

In addition to this answer to prayer, I had many positive developments in other areas of my life. My lawyer gave me good reports about the assault case against me. I went to all the people whom I had beaten, knelt in front of them, told them I had changed, and was now doing God's work. I asked each one of them to please forgive me for beating them, and even offered them the opportunity to beat me if they wanted to! My entire approach to life became much more positive, and I was truly a happy man.

I had been praying for six months by that time, and without anybody to train me, I was still beginning to succeed as a strongman. I knew that was because of the special favor of God. I felt assured that He had forgiven me and was approving of me, and blessing my efforts. I was reading the Bible regularly, and was beginning to understand that He really loved me.

As these things were happening in my heart, I had unexpected opportunities in my outward activities too. One opportunity came from a benefit cricket match in Bangalore that was organized by celebrities for charity. I was hired by the organizers to work as security. As I was lingering with the players one evening in order to entertain them, one of my friends suggested I show them some of the unusual feats that I could do. I performed some that I was already familiar with, but each time I did one that I knew, someone would suggest a new act as a challenge. Amazingly, I was able to do each new challenge!

That night, because of the popularity of the people present, some media crews happened to be there, and they started recording my small performances. Their reports hit the papers and the news the next day, and overnight I became famous. All of a sudden, I began to get many invitations and a lot of media exposure. I became popular and well known all over the country.

After the six months of asking the Lord for those three things, and beginning to get to know Jesus as Lord—and another six months of getting a lot of invitations and publicity—I was invited to my hometown to be honored by my state. I went to Raipur, where my parents lived, and was received with great honors. Even the governor of the state met me and congratulated me. The television and radio news crews surrounded me and interviewed me about my achievements.

I had a lot of different appointments and was kept busy there for about a month. I was very happy to be acknowledged by my hometown, but the best reward was that my father also got some attention and was happy about my achievements. My father said in one interview, with tears in his eyes, that he was proud of me.

Soon after that, in one of the quiet moments I was able to have with my father, I told him of my faith in Jesus. I explained that I had become what I was only because of the answered prayers to the Lord Jesus. I told him that Jesus is the one who made me a strongman and who helped me to use my strength in a good way.

My father responded by asking, "Wait, does that mean that you will not come with us to our temple?"

I thought about it and remembered the teaching in the Bible that we are to honor our father and mother, and I replied, "I am very happy to be here with you, and I will come with you to the temple."

One week after that my father planned to go to the family deity's temple and I accompanied them. It has 1,200 steps, and I climbed up those steps praying only to Jesus in my heart. I did all that they required me to do, but only outwardly. I was thinking only of the Lord Jesus and praying to Him the entire time.

I used the opportunity of a rest on the hill to tell my father that I did all of this to please him, but that I prayed only to Jesus in my heart. He was very quiet, and I knew I touched his heart by what I had done to honor him. He never asked me to do it again. Besides that, even though he is still a Hindu, whenever he visits us in Bangalore he comes with us to our church and attends all the meetings I go to. One of my two younger sisters is a Christian with her husband as well. Many other friends and relatives close to me have also been influenced by the change in my life and have come to know and love the Lord Jesus.

You can see that all three prayer requests were answered. I did become the strongman of India. *Before*, no one liked me. All of my relatives were sad and ashamed of me. My immediate family didn't even want to talk to me or be with me. Now, when I go out, a lot of people want to see me! They want to be with me and have their picture taken with me. The TV stations and newspapers very often cover my performances in India or Asia.

Truthfully, many people are stronger than I am, eat more, and have bigger muscles. In spite of this, they cannot do the feats of strength I do. That is because I do it with the power of God. I was born in a Hindu family, did a lot of wrong things in my life, and even went to jail, but when I gave my heart to Jesus Christ He forgot all of that, saw my heart, and made me a strongman in my own country.

You can see from my story what happened when I began praying to Jesus and recognized Him as my God, but there was so much in me that had to be changed. It was a long, slow process. I had lived a life of pleasing myself in doing all that I wanted, and I hurt many people in the process. I had used my strength to threaten people, and even cheated some. Even though I knew my mistakes and regretted every wrong after committing it, I never thought or desired to stop my actions and come out of that cycle until the day when I prayed to Jesus. With the experience of using my strength for good results—with the goal of a championship and using the opportunities of being looked up to by young people to share Jesus Christ with them—I have had the motivation to change. As the years have gone by, I have come to know more and more about the Bible and God, and my nature has gradually changed along with it.

Revelation

It does not matter where you start in life. It is where you finish life that counts.

Your walk with God will be a process, full of stories of success and failures. Your main goal is to stay humble, obedient, and keep moving forward.

As you follow God, He will take you places that you would have never imagined, to do things that you would have never thought possible.

Application

Share your faith with people of other religions. You never know what God will do, and where He will take that person.

Write down the lies you hear from other people, and even from your own head, then pray God's promises over them. Then tear them up.

Pray and come in agreement with someone who champions you and your dreams in God.

BISHOP FREEZE
www.bishopogfreeze.com

Bishop Freeze: Impact the World CD Coming Soon
"I can do all things through Christ who strengthens me." Philippians 4:13

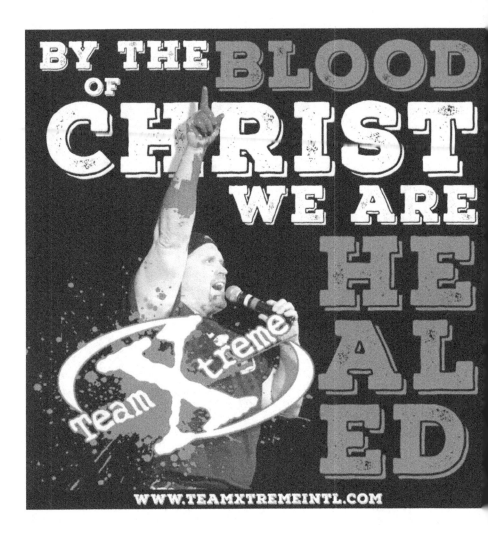

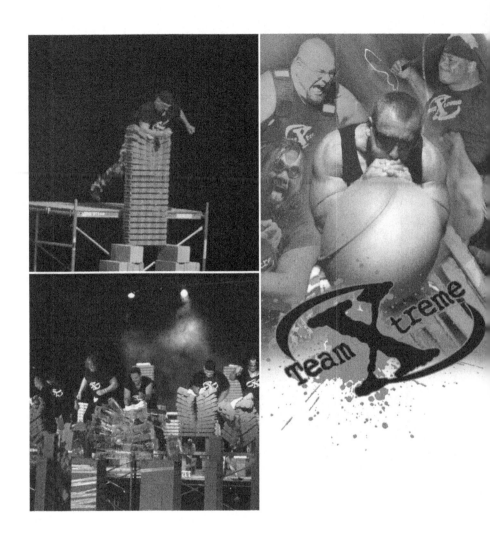

Chapter 11: The Story of the Team Xtreme Ministry Home
Sandra Kenney

Not every adventure that Team Xtreme has been part of involves a "suddenly", or obvious and immediate supernatural provision from the Lord. Sometimes, we have to wait for the Lord's answer, and it isn't always immediately obvious.

For about 2 years, Laura Stark, wife of Kevin Stark (Director of Team Xtreme), was working with various people to get a ministry off the ground. This ministry would help people who believed they were called to serve the Lord, outside of the marketplace, to raise money for their support. Laura had different names for this ministry, but the idea was always the same. She knew so many people that the Lord had called as full-time missionaries, but they didn't know how to raise funds to support themselves and eventually gave up. She didn't know of a single place in all of her years of ministry, where people could go to a physical location to get the training they needed, to learn how to raise money to help them continue to pursue what the Lord had called them to do.

After hearing about this, and praying with Laura in our prayer group, we developed a plan that had multiple objectives. We called it the "three-in-one". Kevin and Laura wanted an office, a house for staff to live in, and a ministry location to train those needing to learn how to raise money. They already had a home, but it was not a good fit for this "three-in-one". They didn't have a timeline on when this would all unfold, but we began the adventure of looking for its fulfillment in the beginning of 2011.

The following is the multi-phased story of how the Lord fulfilled Laura's desire. It is a clear lesson in perseverance when things don't fall into place so quickly or easily.

As her real estate agent in this process, we put the first contract on a house in July of 2011. It was in downtown Grandview, Missouri, right off of Main Street. We found out there was another bid on that house, and the owner decided to go with the other offer, much to our dismay.

It didn't seem like a very good start, but we began looking again. I was asking Laura what she saw in her heart, and she wasn't sure. However, as we kept looking, we seemed to be able to enter into a process of elimination. She knew at least which homes were NOT in the dream of her heart!

The second house was on Skyline Drive, and Laura thought this one would work—the same way she felt about the first one. We placed a bid on it, and this time multiple offers were made. We found out someone else had the highest bid, and they got that house. Oh well. We were learning about bidding wars anyway.

We put a contract on a third house in September of 2011. It was really close to the Global Prayer Room of the International House of Prayer. Even though it had foundation problems in the garage, it had a good layout. But… We lost that bid to a buyer with a higher offer again!

Laura and I were starting to get frustrated after these three failed attempts. It just didn't seem like the Lord was hearing us. We kept praying and looking, but Laura may have been getting frustrated with me too. I didn't want the purchase price to be too high so that there would be some value left in the home if the time came to sell it.

Then there was the fourth house on Red Bridge Road in south Kansas City. I put an offer on this house, but the owner wanted too much for it. We ended up not doing anything with it because the owner wouldn't accept our offer. That house actually never did sell, and the owner ended up renting it out.

The fifth house (which I will designate as 13009 for the address on it) wasn't quite as straightforward as the ones described so far. This home backed up to what used to be the garage but had since been converted into another house. We first looked at it on September 28, 2011. I called the owner and made a verbal offer, but he rejected it.

This was actually the sixth bid I had made for Laura. I made one earlier on this same house, which I didn't mention previously, because after I made it I rescinded the offer. After first making the bid, my husband and I looked at it more closely along with some contractors.

13009 needed extensive repairs and remodeling, and I wanted it to be kept within the market for resale value. Factoring in what the renovation would cost, I didn't think it would be a good value. After I rescinded the initial offer, the price was lowered, but still no one seemed interested because of the same misgivings I had about it. We continued looking, but thought we should keep an eye on this house.

While looking at other properties, and watching 13009, we began to notice several interesting things about 13009. We discovered it was built in 1948, the same year Israel became a nation. It was on lot 22, which is the "double-double" as we call it. It was on 12th Street, and 12 is a number which is representative of government biblically. It had two homes, even though the garage that was converted to a home wasn't very livable. It also had a "double do" room. We were told the first time around that this room had to be torn down and then rebuilt, which was why it was called the "double do" room.

In spite of these observations, the fact remained that 13009 needed extensive remodeling, including replacing knob and tube wiring, moving walls, and plumbing. It just didn't seem practical, so we kept looking.

Laura and Kevin were gone a lot on their mission trips. While they were traveling, I would look over houses in Grandview. When they would get back, Laura and I would get in the car, and I would show her my top picks.

She would say, "I'm not feeling it." Or, "I kind of like this one." We would pray and drive, keeping the adventure and the dream progressing.

The seventh bid I made was on a house that was not close at all to downtown Grandview, but it did have the advantage of having four garages. It was also a really large house. Even though it wasn't that great of a location, given the great square footage, I wanted to put an offer on it. I needed Kevin and Laura to be available for that, but they were out of town and we lost it to another bidder.

Finally, on December 4, 2011, Laura called me and said she felt like 13009 was the house she wanted me to pursue. I called to check on its status. The agent said the sellers were at the title company signing all of the papers for the house, and it had sold! Laura was disappointed, but she was trusting God. We prayed together about this feeling she had, not understanding why the Lord had prompted her. She said that she never wanted to get ahead of God, but wanted to stay right where He is—no matter how frustrating it got—and it was getting really frustrating!

The very next day, after finding out 13009 was sold, the realtor called me and told me the buyer didn't show up! He said, if we still wanted the house, we should let him know. I called Kevin and Laura right away, and we decided to put a verbal offer on 13009. This verbal offer was $20,000 lower than our initial offer, but apparently the timing was right, and the offer was accepted! This was the SECOND verbal offer on the house, and at that point, we began to notice the double theme that was on this house. This became more apparent in the days ahead.

We tried to close on the house December 14, but we were not able to because of a discrepancy with the finances and additional costs, which I hadn't expected. We worked through those problems, wrote an amendment, and came to an agreement. The next day we had our SECOND closing on the house. Kevin and Laura were now the happy owners of the Team Xtreme ministry house!

Early in January of 2012, I felt the Lord prompt me to pick up a toy army man and take it to the new Team Xtreme house. I asked Kevin what he saw when he looked at this toy soldier. Kevin said he saw a "Team Xtreme guy with vision" (the army guy was holding up binoculars and looking through them). He had one hand raised, so Kevin said he saw the TX man praising the Lord. Because the binoculars were a DOUBLE set, Kevin said he saw DOUBLE vision. We positioned the little plastic figurine on the window sill as he kept watch.

Now that the Starks owned the house, we needed to get to work on it. My husband helped me with ideas on the layout, and suggestions for the best ways to change things. I started meeting with Laura and coming up with ideas on how to make the house fit her needs and dreams. We started recruiting volunteers and pulling a house layout together that was practical.

On February 15, 2012, TWO volunteer carpenters met with Kevin, Laura, and me to discuss remodeling. Dave Simmons and Glen Williams ended up becoming a great DOUBLE team! They oversaw all of the volunteers, put in countless hours, and blessed so many people. They had enthusiasm and a great sense of humor as they took us all through the process.

At one of the initial meetings, we were looking around at how to change the layout, and I grabbed something up in the closet that was hidden and nailed to the floor. It was an old tin with a "Safeway" sticker on it, and TWO rings fell off the top of it. One was a high school ring and the other was a wedding ring. They both were so old, but we figured they meant something. On this same day, a dumpster and the "Johnny on the Spot" were dropped off. Shortly after this, a few of the Team Xtreme members moved into the house.

The pipes burst, the sump pump broke, and more things started going wrong. We realized that the inside of the house needed almost everything new, including plumbing. We learned really fast that the warranty company was going to become our new best friend. The plumbing was so old that the company replaced $3000 worth of it. We had to pay the rest, which wasn't much over that amount, to re-plumb the entire house. It hadn't started off too well, but over the next few months a miracle happened.

The volunteers started on February 18 by gutting the house. The carpenter "double-team" had created momentum, and many volunteers regularly came to help out with the many things that needed to be done. One of the first things accomplished was removing the carpeting. After that, the entire kitchen was torn out so we could change its location.

The "double do" room needed extensive remodeling. We needed to move walls to make the layout practical for what Laura had in mind, and the knob and tube wiring had to go. This has since turned into a wonderful room where they now hold ministry and fundraising meetings. Some of the YWAM teams even practice their routines for outreach there.

On June 12, 2013, Kevin and Laura moved all of their things into the house, and they were home! The house they had been living in was sold right around the time the ministry house was ready to move in to. It was a long process, sometimes with little outward evidence of God's leading us. Looking back though, we see the incredible journey and the evidence that God led us through it. Laura never let go of her dream, and it was wonderful to see her dream become a reality.

Revelation

In Acts 2:17 it says, "In the last days it shall be, God declares, that I will pour out my Spirit on all flesh, and your sons and daughters shall prophesy and your young men shall see visions, and your old men shall dream dreams."

God's timing is not always our timing, but His timing is always perfect to fulfill His promises and purpose.

Often what seems like a delayed promise has a purpose behind it, which could include the testing of our faith or shaping of our character.

Application

Ask the Lord to clarify for you what the dream He wants you to pursue looks like

Share your dream with one or two others whom you trust to help you in not giving up.

Continue to ask, seek, and knock regarding your dream.

Feed on God's word and His faithfulness by daily reading, and praying the Scripture, so that you will not lose heart when things seem like they are not going the way you think they should.

Chapter 12: Like Father, Like Son
Tua Meafua

Being a father of three kids and husband to one wife (the only one!) is a God- given gift to me. Just saying "I do" is not the end, though, it requires commitment. This commitment flows out of the decision I made eleven years before I married my wife to believe in Jesus Christ and become His follower. By making that decision, I also gave Him control of my life, but that doesn't mean I am a perfect human being. Jesus was, and is, the key to my life. He is the foundation to overcome any situation, no matter how big or how small.

I grew up in a small island in Samoa. Our culture is very much about being a family and doing things together. It applies not just to the immediate family, but also to the church, village, and larger community. My role models were my parents, grandparents, and all my uncles and aunties, whether good or bad.

My primary role model was my grandfather. He was a hard-working, well-respected man in our village and church. He spoke out openly about what was right and wrong. I looked up to him and carried on some of that responsibility, especially because I was the oldest son of eleven children.

Now that I am a father and a husband, I believe my job is to make sure my wife and kids are safe, and to fulfill my responsibilities as a father. These include responsibilities for the physical, emotional, and spiritual well-being of my family. As I said earlier, it requires a commitment, and it is a full-time job to be the head and the leader of the family.

My wife and I had a baby girl right away. A year and a half after our first girl was born, we had another daughter. Both of them were very big babies: 10.5 pounds for the first girl, and 9.5 pounds for the second one! My wife Patty experienced a long and very difficult labor for each girl, and she had to have C-sections for both of the births. I went into the operating room to watch, and almost passed out!

105

We wanted more children, but after those difficult births, Patty and the doctor closed the door on having more. We still had two beautiful girls, but no son. I thought that maybe we could adopt a boy someday, but I didn't know how or where.

A Son Coming Home
During a visit home to Samoa, I found out that my sister would soon become a single mom. I immediately felt sad for her. I am the older brother of nine sisters, and she is the youngest of the nine. I felt I should talk to her about how I would love to take the baby in, and raise him or her up as the father.

Traditionally, in Samoa, a baby born under those circumstances would end up with the birth mother's mother or older sister, not the birth mother herself. My sister agreed that I would take the baby as my own. At this point, no one knew whether the baby was a boy or girl. A few weeks after my visit to Samoa was over, they called us and said my sister had given birth to a baby boy!

We gave him the name, Benjamin Mataio Meafua. Two months after he was born he arrived in our home, sweet home. We had a son! All of that took place 19 years ago.

Being a Father to My Son
Every day when I looked at him I never thought of him as my nephew. He became my one and only son right from the beginning. As we moved around as a missionary family, it was not easy for our children. Just as they would adjust to one location, we would move again. This happened every few years, but when we moved to Hawaii we were able to stay a while longer. Hawaii is the primary place where our three children were raised, where they went to school, and made friends.

We moved again in 2004 to Utah, and spent 8 years there. During the time we were in Utah, my son turned 11 years old. He began to make discoveries and learned a lot just through living, but also through sports.

As for sports, I was the father that was at EVERY game, and EVERY practice, letting him and everyone know how much I loved and was committed to my son.

I travel a lot for my ministry, but one thing I always said to my son was, "When your dad is not home, your job is to take care of your mother and your two sisters."

This is the tradition in Samoa. The boys take care of everyone in the family, and they have many other responsibilities as men. I wanted to train my son in those ways and to let him know about the importance of being the only son in the house.

Through Thick and Thin
Life is not that easy as a missionary parent following Jesus—even though we get to preach all around the world, see miracles, and watch people being changed for God.

God knows what is best for people, and that includes my own son. We grew in our love for each other and got very close, but as he got older and began to make other friends, he got into trouble at school. I began to worry a lot and became very concerned for him. We did what most parents do: we gave him some discipline, prayed for him, and talked with him. Sometimes that worked, and sometimes it did not.

His behavior got worse, and worse. He did some things that I had never done in my whole life, but I still told him that I would never, ever, give up on him. I wanted him to know that no matter what he did, I was still his father, and I still loved him even when he made mistakes and failed.

I did not worry about my reputation as a missionary. God knew my heart for my son, even when he got to the terrible point of having to go to court to be punished for something he did.

As his father, I looked him in the eye, and said," No one else can change you, Son. Only you can."

I cried, and cried, but I told him something that I felt about him—that one day he would tell his story to many people.

Youth Camp

One day, out of nowhere, my son came to his mother and me. He said he would like to go to a youth camp in Medicine Hat, Canada. We knew some great friends there, and my son's best friend was going to that camp as well.

I took one look at his mother, and she looked at me, and we said, "Let's do it!"

The very next day, we rented a car and drove him up 14 hours to the youth camp.

Two days later, I got a phone call from the camp. There was a move of God the very first night. My son felt the Lord speak to him to go up in front of everyone and share about his life, and to tell them he needed to give his life to follow God. What he shared was very deep, and the counselors wanted to know if I knew about all of the things that my son had been through.

My answer was YES, because I lived and dealt with what he had been through. As a father, I knew we had to love him while trusting in JESUS. We needed to keep the faith and fight for my son's life, just like we fight for the lives of other people that God has called us to reach.

My Best Friend Forever

Now that my son has given his life to Jesus Christ and become His follower, we sometimes tag-team sharing our story. He still has his own dreams, and I want to give all my support to help him fulfill those dreams. He loves his family, and he will do everything he can to protect, serve, and to love others.

What I have learned is to never, ever, give up. Never stop being a loving father to your children. Always try to influence them in a godly way, both in the house and outside of the house. Never try to force them to be like Mom and Dad, but encourage them to become BETTER than Mom and Dad. Now and forever, trust JESUS, for nothing is impossible for Him! Amen!

Revelation

The only way you will succeed in life is to have God at the center of everything—your life, family, ministry, and business. (Matthew 6:33)

Trust God in difficult times. He will make a way for all things to work out for the good, for those who love Him. (Romans 8:28)

Things do not always work out the way you think they should, but know God will work them out the way He thinks they should. Trust His leadership. (Proverbs 3:4-5)

Application

A praying family stays together. Read the word of God, pray, and worship together as a family. If you're not doing that, start today.

Most busy people get to the end of their lives and wish they would have spent more time with their family, and worked less. God, His word, and people are lasting. Everything else passes away. Reset your schedule if you need to, so you have balance with work, family, and God.

Unforgiveness is one of the biggest obstacles to a complete family. When you are the head of your household, ask for forgiveness for wrongs you have committed, and God's blessing will pour out once again.

Bless your family members with verbal blessings. If you have sin that is keeping the blessing of God from flowing, then repent. Ask help from God and other followers of Jesus.

Chapter 13: The Least, the Lost, and the Last
Kevin Stark

As I write this chapter, I am on a flight to Iraq to tell the story of the God-man JESUS, who came to save men of every tribe, tongue, and nation. The Middle East is one of the last frontiers in which to preach the gospel. In Matthew 24:14 it says, "The Gospel of the Kingdom will be preached in the entire world as a witness to all the nations, and then the end will come."

Team Xtreme has a calling to preach the gospel anywhere the Lord opens a door. Some of the open doors have taken us to Iraq, Egypt, Morocco, Syria, Israel, Jordan, and Lebanon. These are tough places where people are afraid to go and share the love of Jesus.

During one of our trips to this troubled area of the world, Team Xtreme was in the city of Jericho. This is the same city we read about in the Old Testament where the walls came crashing down.

We found ourselves in a ramshackle place right in the middle of town. The room we were in was rundown, rat-infested, and full of Muslims. Once again, the walls were about to come down!

We started the show in front of a room filled mostly with Muslim women, who had agreed to attend this weekly meeting of worship and teaching in exchange for a sack of food after the meeting. As we began, the darkness and heaviness in the room was like a thick California fog that was blinding. Instead of playing our regular rock or rap music, I felt the Lord was asking us to play full-on worship tunes.

We did our normal strongman stuff, but we did it to Jesus Culture, Misty Edwards, and Passion. As we praised Him with all of our strength, something like a Holy Spirit bomb dropped and the atmosphere began to change. The heaviness began to come off of people. Anger and fear began to leave and people began to smile, clap, and have fun.

People walking by started to stop and look in, then they started coming in and sitting down. It was as though the beautiful fragrance of Jesus was released, and it drew people to come and sit at His banqueting table. Saed, a born again Palestinian believer on our team, began to share his testimony. A new wave of Jesus' presence came into the room.

Before the show started, Saed was a bit nervous because he lives in the West Bank. He told me that they kill people there for doing what he was about to do. However, when Team Xtreme began this journey of preaching the gospel to the "all and every", we knew it was even unto death if need be. Nothing must stop the preaching of the good news. After sharing our testimonies and preaching the gospel, we asked people to respond to follow Jesus. Many came forward for prayer.

One of the most significant stories was a woman who came asking the simple question, "How do I follow Jesus?"

She was a Muslim woman dressed in a long black gown, and she had several children around her. She began to share a story of several encounters she had with Jesus through dreams. Every time there was a dangerous moment in her life, Jesus showed up in a dream, and warned and directed her. We were amazed at the encounters she told us she had experienced. She had already been following Jesus through her dreams. We shared with her how to surrender and how to worship Him. We explained that Jesus was not just a spirit guide, but her Creator and King. She, and her family, bowed their heads, and gave their lives to our happy God—Jesus.

As the church, together with you, we are called to go after the least, the last, and the lost of the world—even those as difficult to reach as the Muslims in Palestine, or the unreached people groups of the earth. Unreached and unengaged people groups are those who have no witness of the gospel available in their nation.

My friend, Mark Anderson, who founded the ministry call2all, has organized congresses across the world to release the church, missions, and prayer movements to finish the task and usher in the Second Coming of Christ. Team Xtreme is partnering with call2all, along with Impact World Tour, Global Outreach Day, 1Nation1Day, the International House of Prayer, and other like-minded ministries, so that together we can fulfill the Great Commission the Lord gave at the end of Matthew 28.

We recently partnered in an outreach with the Impact World Tour to take the gospel to the first nations people group of the Philippines, called the Ati tribe. The Ati tribal people are among the poorest of the poor and are located in the Cebu Province of the Philippines. We partnered with a local pastor to do an open-air outreach meeting for the tribe. The local church started out with worship, which ushered in the presence of God followed by the preaching of the gospel by Team Xtreme. Most of the tribe was at the event, including the chief. We made a strong call to surrender, and to follow Jesus, but only if they were willing to repent of their sins. We were amazed as we looked out at the people. Everyone responded!

The word of God says that signs and wonders will follow the preaching of the gospel for those who believe. We called tribe members forward for healing. We prayed for the chief of the tribe to be healed of diabetes, and she said she felt a heat running through her body. Another woman was healed, and said she felt light enter her body before her healing. One man, who was filled with anger and bitterness, confessed to murder. Together, with a local pastor, we led him in asking God for forgiveness. We renounced open doors to the enemy, and asked for the Holy Spirit to fill him. Peace and joy flooded his body.

One of the biggest challenges facing the Ati tribe is poverty. Eighty-five percent of the men of the tribe are unemployed with no vision or purpose. This leads to alcohol addiction, crime, and immorality. The Lord gave us an idea to start a micro business with the men of the tribe that would include discipleship and an opportunity for them to start their own businesses.

One simple way of transportation in the Philippines is through the use of a bike taxi. This consists of a simple bicycle with a sidecar for passengers (the taxies are powered by the driver simply pedaling the bike). Income for a day of peddling is only about $5, or about $30 per month. Surprisingly to us, this is enough to live on, and to bring some dignity back into these men's lives.

We decided that, in order to use the bicycle, the driver will first agree to a program of Bible study and life skill training before they take the taxi out. They agree to tithe to the church out of the money they make, and after one year of faithfulness, they are allowed to keep the bicycle as their own. Each bicycle costs only $175, plus $25 for extra parts for repairs.

We don't only want to tell people about Kingdom living, but also to teach them how to live it, and the bike taxi program is an example of this.

One of my favorite stories of reaching the unreached was in regard to two pastors in a Middle Eastern country, who were up all night praying for salvation for their Muslim brothers. In the middle of the night, the doors of their church flew open and several men rushed in to grab the pastors and force them into a car.

As they drove down a long dark road, the pastors figured they were on their way to be killed. They drove up to a mosque and entered a room filled with several men. They were forced to sit in chairs facing these men. One of the leaders began to tell the pastors of a dream that he had. The unique thing about this dream was that each man in the room had experienced the exact same dream!

They said that in the dream, Jesus appeared to each man as they were praying, and told them that two Christian pastors where going to come and tell them the truth about the Kingdom of God. Since no one had come in the several days since they had the dream, they decided to go out and get the only two pastors they knew of.

The pastors were greatly relieved, and they proceeded to share the great news of Jesus, the savior of all nations. Many of the Muslim men who had the dream believed.

This story of these dreams shows that the Lord is actively preparing people to hear the gospel. With His command to go, and His preparation of the people to hear, we can see that the fulfillment of the Great Commission is possible in our lifetime.

By the way, as I type this chapter on the plane on my flight home from Iraq, it is encouraging to report that we just saw several hundred more commit to follow Jesus. The gift goes on. Praise the Lord!

Revelation

Jesus' purpose to come to the earth was to seek and save the lost.

Jesus wishes none to perish, but for all to have everlasting life.

The one who never has heard the gospel should have a chance to hear it and respond.

It is the task of every Christian in the world to fulfill the Great Commission together, not just the pastors.

Application

Ask the Lord how you can be involved with the Great Commission.

Repent for any apathy or indifference on behalf of the least, the last, and the lost. Ask God to give visions on how you can get involved.

Go on a missions trip, or help send someone out that is doing ministry to an unreached people group.

Chapter 14: Xtreme Evangelism
Losi Mahoni

Team Xtreme is not called "Team Normal". Our name reflects who we are inside—"Xtreme" warriors. We often preach the gospel in unconventional ways. We preach the biblical message of salvation, but sometimes we communicate in an extreme way.

Sometimes extreme methods are required in order to get the attention of radical people. I am a warrior from Tonga, and have been a long-time team member of Team Xtreme. I am very loyal, friendly, and faithful, but am also like a wild bucking bronco whose response to things you can't always predict! I have often preached the gospel in unconventional ways with amazing results. Here are six short stories that reflect just a few of the unusual opportunities the Lord has given me to share the gospel with people, and that explain some of my background.

Story 1: A Punch Creates an Opening for the Gospel
We attended the Island Breeze Conference in Tampa, Florida, in 2000. There were people in attendance from all over the world. The theme of the conference was: "Called to Honor Him".

Since the musicians we came with were practicing a lot, we went to pump iron away from the conference center. After we finished working out, we started visiting with some fellows from South Africa. We were all hungry, so I went to the store to buy some food for everyone.

When I came out of the store, there were two guys sitting on the hood of my car. It didn't bother me very much, but I wondered if they were drunk. I put the food in the car while the two guys were just looking at me, not moving. I asked them nicely if they would move so I could go back to Island Breeze. After I got in the car, I opened the driver's door, rolled down the window, and asked again if they would move.

One guy threw back in a deep, mean-sounding voice, with some cussing included, "Come and move me!"

In the past, when someone challenged me like that, I would have fought with him. This time, Jesus was being sweet to these guys through me. I got out of the car, and asked him again nicely to please get off my car.

I think they thought I was scared of them. The big guy sitting on the hood suddenly threw a right hook at my face, but I blocked him with my left hand. I gave him a blow back to his jaw, and he dropped to the ground like he had fallen from the top of a house. It was a hard fall. When he landed on the ground, I gave him a right kick in the chest, and the other guy ran away. This fellow on the ground was trying to catch his breath.

It was almost automatic self-defense to block the punch. I called to the one who was running to come back. He didn't seem to want to, but he did stop, and just stood there with a scared look on his face. He did finally come back, and I helped his buddy sit up. He was finally breathing normally again, but I could tell he was still kind of out of it. I told him I wanted their forgiveness because I did not mean to hurt him. It was just self-defense. They both apologized and asked forgiveness.

I thought they might be robbing people because they both lived on the streets, and neither one of them had a job. After I found this out, I shared with them about my best friend, Jesus, through a story to help them with their situation. They both said, "Yes", to Jesus. I wasn't sure if they meant it, or if they were just saying that because they were afraid of me.

Before they left, I shared my testimony with them of how I grew up on the island with hatred and anger. I hope it helped them. I didn't see the end result, but it certainly was an unusual way to share the gospel!

Story 2: Cussing Gives an Opportunity to Share
While visiting my wife Tracy's family, we decided to go to a local gym together to work out. She went to the ladies' locker room, and I went to the men's to shower. In the locker room, there was a guy cussing, so I turned around to ask how much he got paid to cuss. He looked at me with a weird expression, and did not respond, but continued to cuss. I asked him again if he gets paid for each cuss word, and he said, "No."

I then said that if he didn't get paid, I didn't understand why he was cussing so much, and I started sharing with him about Jesus' love. We were showering together as I shared, and as we got dressed I kept talking about the love of Christ. He seemed to have a lot of pain, frustration, and anger about things in his life. I stayed with him for about thirty minutes sharing about Jesus, and then I asked if he would accept Jesus.

I told him Jesus had a good plan for his life. We prayed together, and I encouraged him, that with his hatred and anger, he needed to get to a good church for help so he could start growing. He thanked me for sharing with him, and for not being too uncomfortable to tell him about Jesus while we were showering. He visibly changed in that short time, and was a lot happier after we prayed. This was a divine appointment to the glory of God—but not an especially conventional one!

Story 3: Alcoholic Father
I grew up very angry because my dad was a violent alcoholic. He tried to fill the void in his life by looking for love.

I responded to this by trying to be a tough guy, and by beating people up. I thought this would make me happy and fill the void inside of me. I thought if I could be the toughest guy around it would make me feel good. I also went to nightclubs looking for women. I thought that if I could find a woman, she would make me happy.

None of that worked of course. I got to the point of hating my life, and this world. I wondered why I had to go through this, and planned on going to the forest to commit suicide. I actually climbed into a tree, was sitting on a branch with a rope tied to it, and put the rope around my neck. I was crying, and was so angry that I was ready to let go of the branch

A thought suddenly came into my mind to pray, but emotionally I did not want to change the plan that I had. Yet, I did start praying, and thoughts started to come that Jesus cared for me, loved me, and had a plan for me. I began to realize that I did not have to take my own life. He already paid a price for me 2,000 years ago, and wanted to take away my anger and stop me from being a bully. He wanted to restore my relationship with my dad as well.

During that time of prayer, I gave Jesus my life, and asked Him to be the Lord of my life—all while sitting on a branch in the top of a tree. I had incredible peace for first time in my life.

He took away my anger, and restored my relationship with my dad. Eventually, my dad repented too, and asked Jesus to come into his life. That's what Jesus did for me, and He can do it for you—but it might not be in a tree!

Story 4: From Robbery to Repentance
I had just arrived in Los Angeles, California, from my home in the Islands of Tonga, and was walking down the street when I received my "welcome" to the city.

I came upon a public phone, and decided to call my parents at home in the islands. As I began talking to my parents, two men began knocking on the phone booth door. It was just starting to get dark. I opened the door, and the two men put guns to my chest and asked for money!

I told them I didn't have any money, and pulled out my pockets to show them. I told them I was from the Islands, and had just arrived here. One of them said, "I am going to shoot you if you do not give me your money!"

I answered by saying that I came to the US to tell people about God and that it was only my second day in the country. Their reply was that they would shoot me if I kept talking about God! Even so, I had a lot of peace and was not scared. I told them, "If you want to shoot me, go ahead."

You see, Jesus Christ is coming back for the people who have their name written in the Book of Life. That is why I wasn't afraid. There is a place called Hell that is reserved for the devil, but if your name is not in that Book of Life, it will also be a place for you.

One of the men said again that he was going to shoot me. I kept sharing Jesus with them, and all of a sudden the gun came down. My mom had been on the phone all this time, and was worried what would happen to me because she heard part of the conversation. I told her I would call her back, and kept sharing with those men for about thirty minutes.

They stayed and listened, and I could feel the anointing and power of God there. I knew I had come to America for a mission and a purpose, and I felt that I was already beginning in it. I told them that Jesus Christ is the King of Kings, and the Lord of Lords, and that it was time for America to turn and worship God.

While I was sharing my testimony with them, and how Jesus changed my life, they started crying. I explained more to them of why I do not have a fear of dying, and I encouraged them to surrender their lives to Jesus and follow Him. I began to lead them in a prayer of salvation. God was touching them and filling the emptiness in their hearts as they asked for forgiveness. I also prayed for them that they would go and tell others about Him, and that He would take their burdens.

119

When I got home, I called my mom back so she wouldn't worry. She had been praying for me.

Two days later, I ran into them in a store. They said they were looking for jobs, and for a church. They ran into me another time later on, and told me they had been blessed with a car from church, and had gotten jobs!

After I moved to Missouri, they contacted me again and told me they had moved to Tampa, Florida. Now they were in a Bible study, and were taking the gospel to the same kind of people they once were when they first "met" me. What an amazing and unconventional thing God did, to use the moment they tried to rob me to lead them to salvation in Jesus Christ!

Story 5: No Toilet Paper Equals Opportunity!
I was in Salt Lake City, Utah, during the 1996 Winter Olympics. I went into the stall of a public bathroom, and found that, apparently, the fellow in the next stall had been waiting for someone to walk in. He was running out of toilet paper! He knocked on the wall and asked if I could hand him some from my stall.

All of a sudden, I thought, "What a great opportunity to share about Jesus!" I asked him if he would give me five minutes to tell him about my best friend. He said he did not want to know about my best friend, so I gave him just one sheet of toilet paper under the stall divider.

He told me that was not enough, so I asked him again to give me just five minutes to share about my best friend. He still did not want to hear about Him, so again I tore off one more sheet and threw it over to him. Of course, he still said it wasn't enough, but finally agreed. "Okay let me hear about your best friend."

I gave my testimony and talked about how Jesus Christ loves everybody. He is a lover, not a hater. We all have so much sin in our lives, and people think they are not good enough. I told him Jesus hates the sin, but loves the sinner.

I said, "Why did God send His son to die on the cross? He sent His only son to die on the cross for you, and He wants to have a relationship with you. He wants to rebuild you." I asked him, "What is your purpose? What is your destiny in life?"

After I shared the gospel, I asked him if he wanted to accept Jesus Christ into his life. He actually said, "Yes!" We were sitting side-by-side in bathroom stalls, and I led him to the Lord! Others walked into the bathroom and wondered what two men were doing just sitting in the stalls, and talking about Jesus! After I shared with him, and he asked Jesus into his life, I gave him a lot of toilet paper!

After we met face-to-face, he wanted me to pray with him again. I told him that everything I shared with him is true—that Jesus is the truth: He had forgiven this man's entire past, and given him His son. What more in this world could he, or any of us, need? God can use anything to show His love.

Story 6: In Brazil with Team Xtreme
Many thousands of people came to our crusade in Brazil. On one particular night, with more attending than usual, Kevin preached the good news and thousands actually came down for the altar call. At the end of the show, we normally pray for people at the altar, but on that night I felt like I was supposed to go into the booth where we had t-shirts for sale.

There were some Brazilian girls in the booth selling ministry t-shirts. One young girl came to the booth, and wanted to buy a t-shirt, but she was short of cash. I asked the girls about her, and they told me she did not have enough money for a t-shirt.

During his preaching, Kevin had given a challenge that if someone listening to him did not believe in God, he or she should go home and ask Jesus if He is real. Kevin said, "I guarantee you He will prove Himself to you."

This young girl was not sure whether or not to go forward and give her life to Jesus, so she stopped by the t-shirt table. We found out later she had asked God to prove Himself to her, and to make Himself real to her if He really exists. Before we knew this part of her story, but after she had prayed—and after the girls told me she didn't have enough money—I opened my wallet and gave her the money to buy a t-shirt. She began to cry! I asked the girls selling the shirts why she was crying, but she answered herself. She said that she heard the challenge from Kevin, and had asked God to show Himself to her if He was real.

Only about ten minutes after she prayed that prayer, the Lord had me there at the right time to give her the money for the t-shirt. I told her Jesus loves her, and that giving her the money for the t-shirt was one sign of His love. She wanted to ask Jesus into her life right then and there.

His ways are far above our ways! He knew that all it would take for her to believe was to have me there to help her buy a t-shirt, and to show her the love of Jesus.

Revelation

Jesus was an "Xtreme" warrior who often shared his message in unconventional ways, breaking religious traditions and mindsets.

Obedience often looks different from what is "normal", and usually goes the opposite way everyone else is going.

Being "Xtreme" is normal in the Kingdom world.

Application

Do not try to be "Xtreme" just to get attention, but pray and tell the Lord you are willing to do anything for Him.

Often people that are in "Xtreme" bondage need an "Xtreme" method to be set free. Do not be afraid to be "Xtreme".

The process of "Xtreme" evangelism takes faith. You have to step out, and then the faith will follow. Ask the Lord to use you daily to rescue broken people.

Chapter 15: Family
Kevin Stark

The auditorium was packed with excited, enthusiastic young people who had come to see GX International, a Christian board, blade, and dance team. Our campaign was in Norway, and it was our kids' debut on stage. Michael was 8, Savannah was 10, and Sasha was 12. The music started, and they began breakdancing with an older dancer named Louie.

Louis was a "popper", a dance style developed mostly out of Los Angeles, but which had spread around the world now. He was the main dancer, and our kids had choreographed a routine around him. They used a line from Psalm 51 for their song that says, "Create in me a clean heart, oh God". As my wife and I saw our kids worshiping God through dance, tears streamed down our faces. We knew then that our decision to follow God by being on the road was the right one, and that God had an amazing plan for each of our kids' lives.

Our family has traveled with the Impact World Tour, a missionary outreach ministry with YWAM that includes the GX International, Island Breeze, and Team Xtreme, for several years now. We have traveled to over 30 countries, and most of the states in the US, preaching the gospel and demonstrating the love and power of God through a relevant presentation.

When we started this journey as itinerate missionaries, we believed the Lord had told us to do it together as a family. This assignment might sound adventurous at first, but after we had been going for a few years, we discovered there was a cost to the calling. We gave our unconditional "yes" to the Lord's challenge to go to the entire world, and to make disciples no matter what the circumstances. This meant going when we did not have the money to go, going when we did not like what we would be eating or where we would be sleeping, going when we were healthy or sick, and even going when our lives could be in danger.

In Luke 9:23, Jesus calls all of us to take up our cross and follow Him. Our journey might sound very difficult to you, but God always gave us His amazing grace and joy to go to the nations. Even though our kids missed out on most of the typical activities of children their own age, they were able to experience the world in a way that most people never get the chance to experience over the course of their entire lives. Our normal family routine was getting on and off planes, homeschooling during the day, ministering at night, staying in host homes, and eating our meals in a local church. We quickly learned that home could be wherever we took off our shoes and hung our hats.

Living on the road has its challenges, but preaching the gospel has bigger challenges. The devil does not like families that are praying together and staying together. He hates it even more when your family is on the road, being a witness for Christ, and following Him well. Spiritual warfare not only became a theology but a revelatory skill that was needed to survive. After a few tests and practice runs, however, you soon learn that you have dominion over the devil, and that living in the Kingdom of God under His leadership is amazing. He won the war on Calvary, and He partners with us to win every battle in our sphere of influence.

We quickly learned that the devil is the father of lies, and if we agree with his lies, then we are bound by them. "Greater is He that is in us than he that is in the world." (1 John 4:4)

The enemy likes to attack the weakest link in the chain, so whether it was my wife, my kids, or me who was having a bad day, the enemy would come after whomever was struggling. Instead of getting angry with that person in their weakness, we would circle the wagons around them, plead the blood of Jesus over them, and watch the demons flee. We quickly learned that "we do not fight against flesh and blood, but against the principalities and powers in heavenly places". (Ephesians 6:12) As a family, we quickly learned how to swing the sword of the Spirit and fight the good fight of faith.

My wife, Laura, is my best friend, my lifetime partner, ministry partner, and a wonderful wife and mother. We made a covenant 29 years ago, and have stayed together for better or for worse (mostly better!), in sickness and in health, and for richer or for poorer.

Over the years of our life together on the road, our covenant with each other was often tested. However, God's grace and faithfulness has kept us in covenant with each other during our times of strength and weakness. God has indeed blessed our marriage. Laura has been a great helpmate, and has sacrificed her life to serve the vision God has given me. Through the years, she has fulfilled much of the vision the Lord has given me, and was strong in the areas in which I was weak. As she has been faithful to serve and follow, the Lord has been faithful to give her the desires of her heart.

Our marriage has been like a canvas the Lord has painted on over the years. In the beginning, we only saw a few broad strokes and did not know what the final picture would look like. As we have kept Jesus at the center of our marriage, we have been able to see God's good workmanship coming into a more complete picture.

Our oldest daughter, Sasha, was born in Hong Kong. She was the first fulfillment of a promise from God—that we would have children who would bring great blessings not only to us but to the nations. With her blond hair even as a little newborn, everyone in Hong Kong wanted to touch her hair and pinch her cheeks. Before we had Sasha, we were just two faces in the massive sea of humanity in that city. However, our new gift from the Lord brought great favor everywhere we went. We believed this was an early sign of the favor that she would carry the rest of her life.

Sasha's name means "helper of mankind". She is fulfilling her calling as she serves the nations in worship, dance, and photography. Her gifts were supernaturally given to her, and she has been developing them to serve her Lord, and the world. Sasha is a beautiful twenty-five-year-old woman now, and she is following hard after Jesus. She is such a blessing to us and to everyone who knows her.

Savannah is our second child. Her name means "treeless plain" in Spanish. She was born in Montana, and carries in her the spirit of adventure and tenacity. She believes that nothing is too difficult for God. Her character exhibits both kindness and a deep confidence of faith. She has had an anointing for art even from when she was young. She has used this anointing for Kingdom creativity in drawing, photography, cooking, and dance. Her merciful heart will be part of her assignment and destiny with the Lord. She shines, and is beautiful inside and out, just like her mother.

Michael is our youngest, and our only boy. His name is from a Hebrew word meaning "who is like God?" I thank God that he gave Michael to me as my son. He keeps the family laughing with his humor and random antics. At a young age, we recognized Michael's athletic and leadership ability as he excelled in soccer and dance.

Michael has a natural ability to lead, and to influence others while just being himself. In the Philippines, on one of our evangelism tours, our son was called on by his team to preach. To everyone's surprise, Michael got up for the first time and preached with great skill and anointing. Many in the room were getting touched by God, crying, and being healed. Destined for greatness through humility and obedience in the Kingdom, he is following God one day at a time. Michael has what it takes to be a real man of God, a great husband, father, and leader.

There are enough stories to fill a book about the adventures our family has experienced together doing missions, but I thought I would share just a few of my favorite ones:

Once, we were going down the road at about 70 mph in the desert outside Taos, New Mexico, and we had a near fatal accident. The car should have flipped over, but by God's protection, we were able to stop our van in the sand. Our kids were very young, and they thought we were playing a game. They were laughing and yelling, "Do it again, Dad! Do it again!", while Laura and I were screaming out the name of Jesus! God protected us many times during our journeys on the road.

Our family has lived by faith for many years by trusting God to provide for what He asks us to do. One of our biggest faith steps was taking our whole family to New Zealand in 2003 for 4 months. We did not have the finances, so we began to pray. We felt like the Lord told us to sell our house, and to use the proceeds for tickets. We didn't know where we would live when we got back, but we knew God would provide.

To make a long story short, a perfect stranger heard about the sacrifice we were making to come to their nation, so they sent us a check for $20,000! We made a $10,000 profit on the house we sold, and someone said that when we got back, we could move into a nice big empty house on 40 acres they had available—for free! Our kids learned many lessons from that trip, but most of all, they learned that God is an extravagant provider.

After most of our shows, we pray for the healing of people's bodies. We have seen thousands of healings over the years. When we were in Gibraltar, Spain, a girl came up to us for prayer for her legs. One of her legs was about two to three inches shorter than the other one. We had her sit down and put her legs together. My kids and I bent over to begin to pray for her leg, and it shot out 3 inches before we could even lay hands on her to pray! We were in complete shock! Everyone screamed, and then praised the Lord! When she stood up, both her legs were the same length and she was totally healed.

One of our most important family lessons was learning how to live in God's presence, and to hear God's voice. We have spent many days sitting in the International House of Prayer, having worship music playing in our house 24/7, or listening to good teaching. When our kids were still very young, we chose not to have a TV in our house. We had movies for the kids, but we felt there were better ways to spend their time than sitting in front of a TV all day. When we asked God what His will was for our family, He guided and directed us.

Even though we have been able to share the gospel with millions of people around the world, our greatest testimony is our family following God together. That testimony continues as our children leave our house, and continue to follow Him with their whole heart.

Revelation

You first responsibility in ministry is the ministry to your family.

Discover your children's gifts and talents, and help to develop them.

Your family needs both quality time and a quantity of time.

A family that prays together stays together.

Application

Evaluate where your family is with the Lord, and began to ask God for His heart and plan for them.

You may have made many mistakes with your family in the past, but today is a new day, and God can forgive past mistakes. He will give you a new destiny for your family.

Ask forgiveness for any past sins toward any family member, and walk out reconciliation as the Lord leads.

Search out the gifts in your children that the Lord has given them, and set a course to encourage them and train them to develop those skills.

Chapter 16: One Nation, One Day
Kevin Stark

"Can a Nation be saved in a day? Can a country be moved in a moment?" (Isaiah 66:8)

True warriors have God-sized dreams that can only be fulfilled if God opens doors and grants supernatural favor. The transformation of a nation seems impossible, especially in these days of political and social correctness. So often, people do not like change, and will resist sudden shifts in direction. The constant promotion of tolerance, and acceptance of everyone's rights and opinions, puts up high walls against change. The only way a nation could be changed in a day would be through supernatural intervention from God.

In history, there have been moments of time when nations have changed in a single day. One such moment was in 1948, when, after 2,000 years away from their homeland, the United Nations granted the Jewish people the right to go back. The nation of Israel was once again among the nations of the world, and it all happened in a day.

Dominic Russo, a friend of mine from the ministry called Missions.Me, had a dream of seeing a whole nation changed by God in a single day. Most great men of faith would likely have difficulty believing that it would ever be possible to change a nation in one day. Yet, to a warrior with a vision from God, nothing is impossible.

Dominic began a five-year partnership with God to see his dream of the impossible become a reality. The nation that God decided to touch was the nation of Honduras. Dominic's cry, from the heart of God Himself, was for a new Honduras. One that would be part of the Kingdom of God—a Honduras in which every sphere of influence would be under the leadership of Christ. Dominic worked and prayed for a new Honduras that would surrender all to Jesus, with the hope that the people would live by the Word of God, and be led by the Spirit of God.

It is not possible in this short testimony to note all that happened, but here are some of the highlights of God's move through the 1Nation1Day vision given to Dominic:

- Two thousand short-term missionaries landed in Honduras for a record-setting short-term mission trip.

- Honduras President Porfirio Lobo declared July 20 a national holiday.

- On that day, simultaneous rallies in 19 soccer stadiums were held across the country.

- The gospel was preached in school assemblies in every school in the nation.

- The main 1Nation1Day event in the nation's capital was broadcast to millions in Honduras, Central America, and around the world.

- 18 industrial containers of food and medical aid were brought in and delivered to the most impoverished areas of Honduras.

- Medical teams of doctors and nurses treated over 20,000 people in 3 days.

- 20,000 pairs of shoes were handed out to thousands of children who had none.

- Two conferences were convened to train and mobilize Honduran leaders to lead the new Honduras.

- 20,000 national volunteers were trained and released for service.

After five days of school assemblies, prayer, leaders training conferences, and mercy ministry, the 1Nation1Day events culminated in the preaching of the gospel simultaneously in stadium venues while being broadcast on national TV. The entire nation was invited to follow Jesus and establish a new Honduras through the Kingdom of God.

After the preaching of the gospel in each venue, an invitation of healing and deliverance was extended, and thousands of miracles happened across the nation all at once. Blind eyes were opened, cancerous tumors were dissolved, people got up out of wheel chairs and walked, and demons were cast out. As a whole nation repented of their sins, a whole nation was delivered from diseases and afflictions that had kept them in bondage for years.

The nation of Honduras corporately cried out for God to come and save them and deliver them, and God was faithful to hear their prayers and redeem them, and establish a new Honduras under the Lordship of Christ.

Walking out the new Honduras will be a process. It will require time and faithfulness, but as millions agreed in one moment to follow Jesus, the question in Isaiah 66:8 that asked if a nation can be saved in a day has been answered.

Can a country be changed in a moment? The answer is, "YES!"

Honduras actually has turned according to the word spoken in 2 Chronicles 7:14: "If My people who are called by name humble themselves and pray, and turn from their wicked ways, and seek My face, then I will hear from heaven, and will forgive their sin, and heal their land." The whole nation heard the Word of God, repented of their sins, and committed to follow Jesus. The heavens opened up, strongholds were broken, the captives were set free, and the Kingdom of God began to be established.

Now that the power of God has been released, the process of establishing the Kingdom of God throughout the nation begins. The Missions.Me ministry, the local churches of Honduras, and many other churches around the world have partnered to ensure that the 1Nation1Day campaign was not just an event. Their follow-up strategies reflect a commitment to make disciples, and to see a nation turn back to God in practice—not just in word—with an initial commitment of a two-year follow-up effort.

This effort is being made through every sphere of influence, using every possible technology and resource. One of the more innovative follow-up methods was facilitated by the gathering of hundreds of thousands of phone numbers during the campaign and venue events. Weekly discipleship text messages are being sent out, along with notices of further training opportunities.

You may wonder what the effect of such a campaign could have on a nation. Here is a sampling of some immediate and dramatic changes we already know about from this historical outreach:

Government data confirmed that, during the 1Nation1Day events, there were no murders at all in Honduras. This is in a nation in which there are typically 19 murders a day.

During the events of that week, the two biggest gang leaders in the city of San Pedro Salas held a press conference to repent of their sins. They asked forgiveness from God, the government, and the people of Honduras on live television. They repented of all the violence and harm they have caused, and they signed a peace treaty. They asked the government for rehabilitation and jobs for gang members.

Two months after the intensive outreach portion of the 1Nation1Day campaign was completed, the government raided the headquarters of the largest drug cartel in the area, confiscating all assets and closing down its entire operation.

While we don't have actual statistics from other events with which to compare, the 1Nation1Day campaign surely ranks as one of the largest and most effective national campaigns ever carried out. Team Xtreme was honored to be a small part of seeing the question of Isaiah 66:8 answered in the affirmative—*seeing a nation saved in a day, and a country moved in a moment.*

Revelation

God is calling the Body of Christ to unite, and to work together to fulfill the Great Commission.

Unity will bring a blessing. The favor and power of the Lord will increase as we are obedient to the Word of God, and the Holy Spirit's direction.

God loves people with faith, and He is looking throughout the world to partner with those who possess such faith.

Nothing is too difficult for God.

Application

Write down your dream(s) in detail, as if you had unlimited resources and power to make it happen.

Discover your purpose. Draw a circle around it, and stay in it for life.

Take risks in life! Where God leads, He will open doors and supernaturally provide.

Write out three "baby step" goals to begin moving toward your dream(s), and a time by which to accomplish them.

Chapter 17: Purity
Cole DeRuse

I am a rapper and a mixed martial artist. I have been with Team Xtreme for two years. Much of what I am about to tell you I have rarely said to anyone. I am going to be honest, open, and transparent because I want you to know the truth about porn addiction, and the destruction it can have on your life. Some of my story is not easy to share, but I believe it is definitely worth it.

My path into porn addiction started when I was 8 years old. I was innocently surfing late night television at my mom's house before going to bed. What I found was not what I was expecting: a came across an explicit adult program. Even at that young age I knew that I should not be watching what I was seeing, but something kept my eyes glued to the screen. That was a night that changed my life for the worse.

My interest in pornography started off slowly at first. If I could get ahold of it through magazines, or watch it on late night TV, I would— but I wasn't pursuing it. (The Internet was not as developed during the late 1990s as it is now, and porn wasn't as readily accessible as it is today.) My fascination really took off in middle school though, right along with my teenage hormones.

I also turned to sexually and spiritually explicit music in middle school as an outlet for my anger. I was angry at my mom for moving away from Kansas City to Montana, angry that my dad and stepmom of eight years were getting a divorce, and just angry at the world. The bus ride to middle school was about 45 minutes, and I could listen to nearly an entire album in that time: Limp Bizkit, Metallica, AD/DC, Eminem, or Jay-Z. Whatever kind of alternative, angry music I could get my hands on I would listen to almost every day. I let the lyrics dominate my thoughts and fuel my anger.

The primary lyrical effect on my attitudes was what this music was saying about women. The songs I listened to said that women were objects of sexual pleasure, and nothing more. I never openly admitted that I agreed with the songs, and I saw myself as a guy who "respected the ladies", but that couldn't have been further from the truth. I was one way in public, but the way I was behind closed doors was an entirely different story.

I was completely preoccupied with my relationships in middle school and high school. I couldn't stop thinking about whomever I was dating. I was always worried about whether or not I had upset them, and wondering if they were mad at me. I was controlling and manipulative, and shouldn't have been dating anyone at all at 13 or 14 years old. I was a hurt and broken boy trying to find his way in life. I was looking for answers everywhere except for where I needed to look—God. At this same time, I was going to Catholic mass with my family, but I didn't really pay attention. Many of my guy friends from school went there too, but we only attended because we had to. We couldn't wait to get out of there and focus on "real life".

Moving on to high school did not improve matters. In fact, my life was deteriorating. I had nearly earned a black belt in karate by then, and was so full of pride. My idol, though, was still relationships with girls. These relationships were deeply rooted in sexual sin and in manipulation of these girls. If I wasn't alone with my girlfriend, I was mad, upset, nervous, and anxious. I wanted only to be alone with her, and to have her focus her complete attention on me. This self-centeredness was nurtured by my ever-increasing addiction to pornography.

Indulging in porn was no longer a once in a while type thing, but it had become a several days a week type thing. My life had been reduced almost exclusively to three activities: if I wasn't with my girlfriend doing things I shouldn't be doing, or training for martial arts, I was behind a computer screen getting attached to fantasies online. I became so attached to some of them that sometimes I couldn't tell the difference between fantasy and reality.

During my remaining years of high school, and after, my relationships continued to go from bad to worse. I was basically a womanizer—texting who I wanted when I wanted—regardless of whether or not I had a girlfriend. I defined cheating as a physical encounter with a girl who was not my girlfriend at the time. Nothing else counted as cheating in my mind. I considered pornography, masturbation, and any other related activity to be fine as long as no one found out.

I worked hard to make sure no one did find out because, during this time in my life, I actually committed myself to Christ. Most of my close friends were from the karate team, and we were all going to church every week.

Even though I had come to Christ, I still lived in compromise with sexual sin. I would let God have anything except this secret area, and predictably, things got much worse. I wasn't in a relationship at this time, so I spent hours online surfing the Internet late at night. I went from just looking, to searching out chat rooms, and more. I couldn't get enough, and all the while I felt fake as a Christian.

Nobody knew, and that was my problem. I was great at hiding things. I would cry out to God for help, and respond to altar calls during church services, but I would never confess my sin to anyone to bring healing. I needed help, and I knew it, but I was too scared to reach out to someone. I began losing sleep because I stayed up way too late into the night engaging in sinful activities. I knew things were going to end terribly if something didn't change soon.

Perhaps some of you who know me may be surprised at this point in my story. You might even be disappointed, hurt, or upset. If you knew me during this time, you knew I claimed to be a Christian and to live for God, all the while I was indulging in secret sin. I was fake and living a huge lie. This is just one of the many things I've done that I'm ashamed of.

I had hurt countless girls by devaluing them and treating them disrespectfully. Just like the message of the music I listened to, I treated girls as objects, not as daughters of the King. I didn't fully realize the damage it would cause to others, and to myself down the road. I felt like it was too late to change, but I knew my sin would find me out sooner or later.

My mind was dominated by sexual thoughts and actions, even while people looked up to me as a new Christian music and martial artist. One of the most difficult things I've had to do in life is to keep up the fake external picture of what people thought I was, but in reality, I was completely addicted and needed to get away from where I was. I needed God to take me out of this lifestyle I had adopted.

He did just that at the end of the summer in 2011.

I was driving home from church one night when I felt like the Lord had told me I was going to be leaving soon. I didn't know what that meant, but I answered, "I'm not sure how, but if you send me I will go."

A month later, I was suddenly laid off from my accounting job with no notice. It was a shock, but God knew that in order for me to leave, I had to have a reason to leave.

A month after losing my job, I was scheduled to rap at a church event. I was to be the opening act for a strength team called "Team Xtreme". I knew that a rapper used to travel with the group, and I was really hoping the team would ask me to tour with them. Believe it or not, it actually happened!

That very night, after we had both performed, they asked me to come with them! They were leaving in four days for a two-month tour in North Dakota, Scotland, and Northern Ireland! I knew this was what I needed—a chance to get away and start fresh. They took me in as one of the team, and they have been discipling, training, and helping me in being raised up by the Lord since that night.

It has been quite a journey, and some days have been extremely difficult. The day I first hopped into the van with Team Xtreme was September 15, 2011. That day I decided to commit every area of my life to Christ. No more games. No more faking. My life was going to be all for God, or nothing.

I was able to confess my sins to them, and to get the help I had desperately needed for almost twelve years. They didn't judge me, but they loved me. They accepted me for who I was, but also called me out as the leader God had always planned for me to be.

It hasn't been easy, but God has put me on a course of coming clean with my friends and family. I also sought forgiveness from the girls I had been with in the past, while learning to overcome my addictions and mindsets that had plagued me for so long. It has been a process of surrounding myself with people who love the Lord, and learning to live a life of accountability and transparency.

This would already be a wonderful story to this point, but it isn't quite finished. In fact, the best part is yet to come! The same day I jumped into the van with Team Xtreme is the day I met Danelle Dunken. That day was her first with Team Xtreme as well. We had more than a ten-hour van ride to North Dakota, so I had some time to meet the team and get to know them. Danelle really stood out to me as a woman of honor, integrity, and PURITY.

The purity I saw in her was new to me. I was very attracted to her virtue, and knew that I wanted to live my own life of godly integrity and purity. After getting to know her just a little in that long van ride, I realized that if I ever was to marry someone, I would want it to be to a girl like Danelle. That very night, we attended a conference to begin the tour in North Dakota.

Again, everything changed for me that night in the best way possible! First, God called me into the mission field full-time that evening. On top of that, He told me two different times that night that Danelle was going to be my wife! Yes, it was weird, and I didn't believe what I was hearing. I thought I was crazy, but I eventually shared it with the leaders of Team Xtreme. I definitely did NOT share it with Danelle. That would have been an awkward way to start a relationship!

As time went on, we became great friends. It was so refreshing to get to know her for who she really was and not just for her looks. During our first year of getting to know each other, we remained "just friends". We both knew we had feelings for each other, but we wanted to seek God's timing and not our own.

At one point, I felt convicted by the Lord about having an emotional relationship with her. I was only texting and talking on the phone with her from time to time, but I broke things off completely. Before I gave my heart to someone else, I first wanted to give my entire heart to God. I wanted Him to repair it and give it back. That way I would have a whole heart to give to somebody else when the time was right.

When I felt like the time was right, I took Dani on our first date to have her pray about entering into a courtship with me. I was so nervous, but I also had peace from God, and the go-ahead from the leaders of Team Xtreme and my missionary base. That night, I told her how I felt, and asked her if she would pray about entering into a relationship with me. In the meantime, I called both of her parents and got their blessing before going forward into a relationship.

August 26, 2012 was the day our relationship began. It was a great start to a new and exciting season. From the very beginning, we set boundaries and guidelines with which to be held accountable and never to cross. I wanted to do this right. I wanted to treat her with respect, and above all, I wanted to honor God through it all. We set a curfew for date nights, agreed never to hangout alone behind closed doors, and agreed to pray together every day and night. It was a learning process that was not easy at times, but it was so worth it!

After much prayer and reflection, I proposed six months later. I had already prayed things through with my spiritual leaders, and had the blessing of her parents. The engagement story is more than I have room to write, but I can say it was a complete surprise, and she never saw it coming! Just to give you a little flavor of it, I saved the letters I had written to her over the past year, and encoded in them the message, "Dani, will you marry me?" We decoded it together on February 9, 2013, with her back to a whiteboard and me having played the role of Vanna White!

Four months later we were married. It was an amazing day! A very special part of this was that we saved our first kiss for the wedding day—June 15, 2013! We waited because we believed it was worth it. I wanted to make sure I didn't mess up this time. I wanted Danelle to know her value, and how much she meant to me, by waiting until marriage for physical intimacy. This was new and different for me, but God gave us much grace, and we were able to become the best of friends before marriage. I wouldn't have done things any other way!

God has used our testimony of patience and purity to impact people across the globe. I've been able to share my story to challenge the youth of today that it is okay to wait—that women deserve a man who will treat them with respect, and that guys can have what it takes to be a man of godly integrity.

I'm not perfect. You can easily see that by reading my story. Statistically, I shouldn't be where I am today. However, God's grace covers my life, and He has set me free from my former secret lifestyle. My story is now out in the open for my close friends and my wife to know. They pray for me, challenge me, keep me accountable, and help keep me committed to living out a Job 31:1 lifestyle. (See the verse in the "Application" section below.) The temptation to fall back into an addiction to pornography is still there, but it is not nearly as strong as it used to be.

Every day I have to choose to believe the Word of God, and use it to renew my mind. I want to stay faithful to my wife. I want to have a family someday, and I refuse to become a statistic of divorce. We actually stated in our wedding that the word "divorce" would not even be in our vocabulary. Keeping God front and center will enable us to live out a continued life of purity.

Revelation

Your past does not define your future.

No matter how "dirty" you think your life is, turn back to God. He will take you in and clean you up.

Confession of sin brings healing, and will play an important role in your getting free.

Love is patient. Saving physical intimacy for marriage is God's plan, and will save you from much heartache.

Application

Don't merely give God some areas of your life, but give Him everything.

Find someone you look up to and trust, such as your pastor or spiritual leader, and share with them your struggles. Don't hide the truth. Come clean. Confession is the key to seeing your healing come forth.

Set up safeguards with an accountability partner to help you maintain a life of integrity and purity.

Job 31:1: "I made a covenant with my eyes not to look with lust at a young woman." Find and memorize scriptures like this that will help combat temptation during moments of weakness.

When you mess up, run TO God, and to your accountability partners. Everything inside of you will want to hide it and run away. Remember that a true warrior rises to the challenge of making decisions that take courage, heart, and dedication. You CAN do it. Keep pressing!

Chapter 18: Miracles in Media
Thure Erikson, TX Vikings

Backstage, a half hour before our *Norway's Got Talent* performance, there were a thousand butterflies in my stomach. We were all praying in the Spirit, but scared to death in the flesh. We heard a call from the show's emcee saying, "They are very Christian and very wild!"

Jesus had already begun His transforming work in our lives before this show. We were just a bunch of nobodies going nowhere before we met Jesus. We had all been criminals, drug addicts, or gangsters—full of hate and pain—but now, the music was starting! The door into the realm of media had been opened by God, and it was about to change our lives forever.

We knew there would be roughly one million people in Norway watching this show, or about 20% of the population of our small country. Even greater numbers of youth—about 40% of all the young people in the country—would be tuning in. As we prepared for the show, we agreed that we did not want to hide Jesus and the gospel, but we wanted to do a show that explained the entire story of His good news.

As Vikings of Norway, we have a history and carry a reputation of being violent brutes who love to break things. Jesus showed us a way we could use this background and reputation to preach the good news, and to be faithful to our agreement not to hide His story. We used the theme from "Mission Impossible" for the opening song, to emphasize that the mission of life is possible because of the finished work of Christ, and then we started the show by breaking a six-foot stack of ice.

As it broke, I said, "The ice and the heart of the Father is broken for you. The wall of ice stands for the wall of sin and death that was broken, and now we have been given the Spirit of life, as Romans 8, verse 2 says."

144

All the rest of the show, we used visual illustrations to explain aspects of the gospel, and an upbeat song by Carmen to give a good background. We broke two sticks over the backs of two team members, demonstrating the stripes Jesus took for the healing of our bodies that was foretold in Isaiah 53:5. We broke baseball bats, and put them up in the shape of a cross. We did this while talking about Calvary and how He was beaten and suffered, demonstrating His love for us and His willingness to be the sacrifice of sin in our place—as in John 3:16. We broke another stack of bricks with the word "freedom" painted on it.

One of our Vikings hit it with his fist, and yelled, "Freedom! After the blood of Jesus covers you, you are free from the power of sin and death. All the walls of sin have to come down, just as it says in John 8, verse 32."

At the very end of the show, we had two 250 lbs. logs we lifted over our heads. One log represented Jesus, and the other the Father.

When we lifted the logs, we said, "As you follow Him, He will lift you up in His joy and peace."

We then set both logs on fire and said, "The fire represents the Holy Spirit, Who gives you the power to live a supernatural life in the Kingdom of God."

Then, I ran through two 2x4 pieces of burning wood, and said, "There's breakthrough for you tonight!"

The show ended on that dramatic moment.

As it came to a close, the emcee said, "For the first time in my life, I understood the gospel completely."

We used four minutes for our show, and the time went very fast. Who would have thought we could do a four-minute gospel presentation? Contestants on the show are only normally allowed two minutes, but we had favor, and the producers of the show gave us more time. I felt that the Holy Spirit's assignment for us, in those four minutes, was to present the full gospel to the whole TV audience.

The emcee asked, during our interview after the presentation, "What are you feeling?"

I said, "I feel very happy!"

She attributed our happiness to the show's having a lot of testosterone in it, but we all knew it was the presence of God.

I then yelled out, "Who is in the house?!"

The guys all replied, "Jesus!"

I was very happy and satisfied with the results, and was amazed we had the opportunity to preach the gospel to the Norwegian people on national TV. I know of no one else who has been able to preach the gospel to the whole nation of Norway before. On top of it all, we ended up as one of the ten semifinalists in the show.

During the process of qualifying for Norway's *Got Talent*, God opened up many doors for us to witness to the judges, producers, and other contestants. One of the judges had been on the panel on these kinds of shows in other countries, and was usually very mean to the contestants. I told him at the audition that we used to be very mean and beat people, and I told him I knew he was also mean.

Even so, after the semi-final show, the judge said, "This is a mixture of a freak show and a Jesus kind of show, but after watching, I can see that you have talent."

Another judge who is a standup comedian said, "This is what the state church in Norway needs."

The third judge said, "You look like you are mean, and have muscles like mountains, but inside you are like beautiful pussy cats with a good message. I come from the Lutheran Church, but you have a clear Jesus relationship. I can tell."

Media and Team Xtreme

When, and how, did I get the vision to go into media for ministry? It started when I met Kevin Stark, a great man of God. He had a team called Sports Excellence, and he told me that I should start a team like his in Norway. I told him that Christians in Norway don't do sports skills because they are too religious.

Then God called me very clearly at the end of 2003. Early in 2004, I began following that vision, even though I was all alone. When the Lord said, "Now you go," I knew I had to go.

I went to a store to buy materials, and met Alex. He had done some work on my house before, but I didn't know him really well. I pointed my finger at him and asked, "Are you ready?" He said he was. I recruited four more guys.

We did some shows, but nothing much happened until the Lord said to me, "You have to learn to walk in My love for one another, and have relationship with Me. Learn to be in Christ's unity, and live in the light."

That is when He turned the voltage on, and God's power started manifesting. Kids were coming to Christ, and God was healing people.

Later on, the Lord said, "I want you to go to the media. Not the Christian media, but to the national TV stations."

In 2006, we started out with TV Norway doing some talk shows. They were good programs, but the Lord wanted us to go to the masses. TV Norway also had some local stations. The head guy saw us, and wanted the same program clip on the main channel.

They got clips of us, but we didn't get a call. So, we prayed for two days. After praying, TV 2—the main station—called us and put us on the six o'clock news. This was also when they invited us to be on *Norway's Got Talent*. They told us they asked because they didn't just want singers, but wanted a more colorful program. I told them we were not in the entertainment industry, but in God's ministry. If they wanted us in there, they should know that we were going to preach Christ. They agreed.

We try to be unique, and to do things that are outside the box of religion. Most people in Norway do not go to church, but they all watch TV. People who watched the show thought it was cool. Many churches today try all kinds of things to get people into church, so they thought it was great to preach the gospel on TV. This sort of thing doesn't happen in Norway, Sweden, or Denmark. It was a breakthrough for us to be on the show.

There was a production company with NRK (the Norwegian Broadcasting Corporation) and TV 2 who wanted us to do a documentary, and some reality shows, but they wanted us to do them with their slant on the shows. That is not our vision from God with media. We must do shows only from His perspective.

We didn't give up, however. We searched for the right person from those production companies, and now we have the right person. At first, they wanted us to tell about how ugly and disastrous things were for us, sort of like a reality TV show or tabloid newspapers. We do have all kinds of stories like that because we lived the wild life, but that is not the Lord's assignment for us.

When the Lord told us we were going on national TV, I began to proclaim it in the spiritual realm in our team meetings. We stood firm in the Lord's assignment, and didn't go the way the producers wanted.

148

The Lord began to bring the right offers, and we are now appearing on TV in Israel and Estonia too. We are part of their regular programming on a few channels.

Because of our appearance on *Norway's Got Talent,* we have favor with several companies, and we have amazing stories from journalists we worked with in television. Production and camera people now respect the gospel and Jesus because they have more understanding from our testimonies.

One journalist told her cameraman to turn off the video during an interview because she needed to receive Jesus first, and do the interview later. It was while they were filming a documentary about us on tour, and they wanted to put the interview on the 6 o'clock news—just six months after the semi-finals of *Norway's Got Talent.* She was touched, and stopped the interview. The Lord was working in her. She received Jesus right there! She then changed into a more modest dress, and continued with the interview! It has been amazing to watch God open new doors that have not been available before to preach the gospel on TV.

Our most recent open door in media has also been the most exciting. The TV stations in Norway want to film a twelve-week reality show about the TX Vikings, and televise it during primetime. We will shoot the series on an original Viking ship going to ten different ports in Norway, preaching the gospel along the way. Who would imagine that the secular world would want to make a TV series about a bunch of crazy, "xtreme" Vikings who love Jesus? With God all things are possible!

Revelation

Nothing is impossible for God.

God wants to give His children favor and use them as leaders in every sphere of influence.

Authority and power comes with obedience.

Following God will take you places you never expected to go.

Application

Be faithful in the small things God has placed before you, and expect greater things to come.

Write down your vision/dreams, tell people often, and walk out the steps God has placed before you.

If you tried once and failed to go after your dream, recalculate, make Jesus the leader of the plan, and try again.

Chapter 19: Partners
Kevin Stark

At church one night, a friend asked if I knew who Werner Nachtigal was (Founder of Global Outreach Day), and if I would like to meet him. Werner is from Germany and was visiting for the day. The likelihood of us connecting that night was almost impossible.

My spirit jumped inside me. I had been praying for a few years for a day when all of the Christians in the world would come together after the Global Day of Prayer, to go out and preach the gospel, and see millions of people saved. The Global Day of Prayer is amazing, but I thought, now they need to go out and preach the gospel. Little did I know that someone was already doing that through a ministry called the Global Outreach Day. (G.O.D.) What a divine appointment.

Another time, one of our staff came to my house with a brochure called "One Nation, One Day". Again, my spirit jumped inside of me as I looked through the brochure. The Holy Spirit was speaking to me, saying, "You need to be part of this." I had been crying out to the Lord in prayer for years, to see whole nations won over for Him.

Psalm 2:8 says: "Ask me and I will give you the nation for your inheritance, and the ends of the earth for your possession." I have cried out that prayer many times as I stood in front of the map at the Global Prayer Room, believing that there was going to come a day where whole nations would come to follow Jesus. Thus began Team Xtreme's partnership with Dominic Russo and Missions.Me. Since that day with the brochure, we have partnered with Mission.Me in several world-changing initiatives.

Two other partnerships that the Lord connected us with were IHOPKC's Global Prayer Room, and Impact World Tour. The partnership with Impact World Tour has been going for 20 years, and with the International House of Prayer for 15 years. All of these partnerships have been ordained by the Lord as part of our destiny, in equipping and empowering us to be who we are today. As you surrender your vision and your ministry to the Lord daily—as you rest in Him, and wait on Him—He will supernaturally open up the heavens. He will give you divine appointments, providing just what you need (and who you need) to complete what he has called you do.

The partnerships with the International House of Prayer and Impact World Tour really laid down a firm foundation of prayer and preaching into our lives. These partnerships have allowed us to do things that we would never have imagined could happen. We are so grateful to Mike Bickle of IHOPKC, and Mark Anderson of IWT, for setting a table for us to come, learn, and develop our gifts. Through these ministries, we have been all over the world. We have been able to preach the gospel to more than 20 million people and grow in our faith to believe God for the impossible.

Two years ago, I began to pray the prayer of Jabez, that the Lord would begin to expand the borders of our territories. I prayed this prayer almost every day, waiting to see how God was going to make this happen. Through this prayer, the partnership with the Global Outreach Day and 1Nation1Day were birthed. Since I have already talked about 1Nation1Day in Chapter 16, I would like to focus on G.O.D.

G.O.D has only been in operation for three years, but has already seen 15 million people trained and sent to preach the gospel in over 100 nations. The vision of G.O.D. is that everyone can "reach one", and together we can reach the world.

As people go out to preach the gospel, they can do it in any way the Lord guides them. (These include acts of kindness, going out two by two, taking someone for a cup of coffee, or a large group event.) The starting point of G.O.D. seeks to send out every Christian in the world to the lost on a single day, but the ultimate vision is for millions to be trained as evangelists to go out and preach the gospel every day. There have been prophetic words that, one day, over 500 million will be trained and going out at one time.

One of the most amazing testimonies of G.O.D. is from the nation of Nepal. In 2014, 6,400 churches worked together in unity to reach their whole nation. The result was that 100,000 new believers joined churches, and 1,600 new churches were planted.

Another amazing report of the G.O.D outreach was in the nation of the Dominican Republic, where 2,100 churches and 102,000 Christians shared the gospel to more than a million people. After the outreach, more than 70,000 people attended a Bible course. In Brazil, 30,000 churches with an estimated 3,000,000 Christians actively shared their faith.

As we have partnered with G.O.D., we have been training churches on how to evangelize, and then to establish their own evangelism teams to go out and preach the gospel. Our goal is to see each person on an "E-team" share with at least one person every day. We want to see them do some type of group outreach each month, and an international or large event every year, while continually training everyone in the church to be a witness.

As we have been traveling the world and doing ministry, we have seen the Lord bringing the Body of Christ together in unity to finish the task of fulfilling the Great Commission. We work better together, and the Lord will always bless us serving each other and working together. Let us look for ways to come together in prayer, and in similar visions and assignments.

Even though the Lord has opened partnerships with huge visionary ministries the last several years, it has been individuals and small churches that have consistently allowed us to GO to the nations. We always tell people, if it were not for you, we could not do what we are doing. As Youth With A Mission volunteers, every person has to raise their own support, and each ministry has to trust God for resources for operational costs.

You never join YWAM for the money—it is not a strategic career move up the corporate ladder for financial security. We joke about the acronym of YWAM meaning Youth Without Any Money. However, as we are learning to trust God for resources, and to see whole nations transformed, we have changed our way of thinking: to YWAM meaning Youth With A Million.

The priority of partnerships is not about money, but about people that are like-minded, coming together in heart-connected relationships to establish the Kingdom of God on the earth. At first, it might seem like partnerships are centered around sending a check and completing a task. However, as the process of Kingdom partnership develops, you fall in love with each other and the assignments that God allows you to pursue together.

We have friends of our ministry who have been partnering with us faithfully for more than 25 years: giving, praying, and sharing our lives together. We have walked with each through the good times, and the bad times, trusting God all the way.

We have so many amazing partners that if we were to tell the stories of doing life with all of them, it would fill another book. We thank each one of you who gave, prayed, and shared your lives with us. Many will be in heaven because you were obedient. To God be all the Glory, and may the rewards of the harvest be credited to your account.

Revelation

We are the Body of Christ, created by God to work as one body with separate parts.

The devil, and the systems of the world, have divided and weakened the church through, strife, disunity, and selfish ambition.

Unity through diversity can work if we keep Christ at the center, and if our focus is to serve one another and to reach the lost.

Application

Pray for unity of the Church, and repent from any actions of disunity,

Look for ways to partner and serve other visions beside your own. Give financially to other ministries.

At least once a year, get involved in a unity project to reach the lost or serve your city.

Ask the Lord for long-term partnerships that you can collaborate with other churches and ministries on, to expand the Kingdom of God.

Chapter 20: Business with a Mission
Kevin Stark

A vision is a dream co-created by God with his sons and daughters to bring glory and honor to His name, and to establish His Kingdom on earth. Each one of us possess a calling given to us by God, but we also have things we love to do. Put these two things together, and you get your life vision and purpose. In the natural, if your son or daughter has a passion or dream, you will do everything in your power to make it come true.

As a parent, you love to see your children's visions fulfilled. However, out of love for your child, you will never give them something they are not ready for, or that will harm them. If we, as finite humans, have a strong desire to help fulfill our children's destiny, how much greater is the desire of our heavenly father to see his children's desires come to pass?

The Lord loves you, wants to give you a vision, and then empower you to fulfill it!

Oftentimes, a vision can take longer to be realized than we would like. However, God's timing is always perfect, and He often is more concerned about the process than the completion of such a vision. It is through the process of fire that we are strengthened, trained, tested, and prepared for our destiny.

A vision often dies just before it is fulfilled. Sometimes, this is the final test to check the motives of our heart and the Lordship of Christ over our vision. The death of a vision is always painful, but the resurrection that follows is always wonderful and exciting.

Most of these sorts of dreams will have an apostolic leader, and followers of the visionary, who will serve that vision. Servants often are in training to prepare for their own vision one day. Oftentimes, the vision will have a "Jonathan" who will unconditionally serve and stand by the visionary for the duration of it. Jonathan in the Bible was

158

David's armor-bearer, loyal friend, and faithful servant for much of his vision.

My amazing wife, Laura, who has followed me around the world, has been our family's Jonathan. We have spent most of our married life traveling with our children to the nations. We have slept in hundreds of different beds, spent endless hours in boats, cars, taxies, planes, and trains (even on camels… and a water buffalo). We have eaten every kind of strange food imaginable, escaped moments of danger, endured sleepless nights, and prayed for our kids through sickness in strange lands.

Laura has been our family's armor-bearer, loyal friend, amazing wife, faithful mother, and giving servant over the years. She has been selfless in serving not only our family, but also in serving and caring for the vision of many others. Laura is a great networker—not for the purpose of her own agenda, but for the advancement of others. Very few serve like this woman.

As you go through the process of fulfilling your vision, it changes and adapts by the leading of the Lord. This vision always should be big enough that only God can accomplish it, and it should have many ways to multiply and allow a platform for others to begin their journey.

Many ministries have been birthed through Team Xtreme. We currently have more than 20 TX and partner teams around the world. Our desire is to give away the gift God has given to us to as many people as possible.

One of my great desires is to see my wife's vision, the ministry Business with a Mission/We Give Foundation, come to pass. The heart of Business With a Mission is to see the businessmen and women of the world partner with missionaries, and for both of them to prosper and fulfill their callings together. The focus of the We Give Foundation is to see resources released to fund the Great Commission and other Kingdom initiatives.

159

The Old Testament talks about the kings (business leaders) and the priests (spiritual leaders). Both groups have specific gifts and callings that are important to the establishment of the Kingdom of God on earth. For so long, these callings have been separated, and at best, have operated as secondary next to each other. However, we believe the Lord is calling these groups to partner at a new level of unity and focus to bring change on the earth.

The best model of partnership between kings and priests is the Bible story of Nehemiah and Ezra, and their rebuilding of the temple in Jerusalem. Nehemiah was the general contractor and business manager of the project, while Ezra was the watchman on the wall (prayer and worship coordinator), and spiritual developer. They worked together with great skill and focus, complementing each other's giftings and leadership. It is always easier for the priests and kings to do things separately, and for each of us to remain within our own area of expertise—to keep doing things the same way we have always done them. The understanding that every Christian business is a ministry, and every Christian ministry is like a business, would certainly be a helpful revelation to the Body of Christ.

Laura's vision is to gather the kings and priests, and to allow the Lord to connect them—first through relationship and then through purpose. The partnership will grow together, naturally and effortlessly, as the Lord gives each businessperson a mission. In order to fund these initiatives, the We Give Foundation was formed to see resources released to pay for such projects. Currently, we are overseeing funding on more than 35 Kingdom projects. The projects we release funds to are centered around Christian mission, prayer, mercy, and Israel.

Most visions are realized gradually, with periods of opposition, and periods of growth spurts. The main key to success is bathing the vision in prayer, God's presence, and being obedient to God's plan and timing.

Proverbs 16:9 says that a man plans his way, but the Lord directs his steps. Our success in the fulfillment of a vision will be found in seeking God for the steps, and the timing of those steps.

If we look back to the story of Nehemiah and Ezra, we see that a vision was given to Nehemiah, supernatural provision was provided through King Cyrus, and a God project was started. Even though God initiated and provided for the vision, there was great opposition once the project began. Opposition against your vision does not mean God is not in it; more likely, it is an indication that God IS in it, and the devil wants to stop it before it can succeed.

The partnership between Cyrus, Nehemiah, and Ezra was amazing. They all had a common vision, but each one knew their assignment within that vision. As the physical and verbal attacks came upon Israel at the wall, the priest prayed and the kings worked and protected, and at times they all came together to work and pray in unison.

As the vision for Business with a Mission develops, we have seen several partnerships develop beyond the normal king/priest relationship. Phil and Gina Cohan of Cohen Woodworking lead one of the best Kingdom businesses I have ever seen. We have been working with this couple for about a year now, developing our relationship and ministering to their staff and leadership. We have partnered on several initiatives that have advanced the Kingdom of God in both our ministry and their business. I have learned a lot from Phil and the way he leads his family and business.

Phil and Kathy Butler of Kansas City are longtime friends whom we have been walking in life with for a number of years. They have gone through a lot of tough times. In just one month, Phil lost his business, his family, and his relationship with God. After three years of running from the Lord, he ended up in the very jail cell where he used to do ministry. Repenting from his rebellious ways, he was restored to his wife, family, and business. Throughout the journey, we have stayed friends. Since his coming back to the Lord, doors have been opening up to do more Kingdom stuff together.

Sandi Kenney has been a partner with Business with a Mission for 12 years. She and her husband, Bill, have been faithful friends, partners, and co-workers in the Kingdom. We have prayed and believed the Lord for many miracles together, and will continue to seek the Lord on how we can establish the Kingdom of God together.

Karl and Chris LaPeer were one of those sudden divine appointments God will bring into your life, which proves that He is real, alive, and is hearing your prayers. While doing ministry in Peru, I met Karl at one of our meetings. We had a short 10-minute conversation, and he said that God was speaking to him right then and there to significantly fund the work that we were doing. I was amazed... I had just met the man. Since then, the LaPeers and our family have connected in many ways, becoming dear friends and Great Commission partners.

We have had many other great partners in ministry—too many to mention. We thank all of them, and believe the Lord is currently changing the way ministry is being done. As all the spheres of influence come together, seek the Lord on how we can be unified in our diversities. We can do it better together!

Revelation

> The earth and everything in it is the Lord's. God sees everything in a holistic perspective, but man wants to divide everything into compartments. To change the world, we need to understand that we must bring the Kingdom of God into the different areas that control the nations. This includes church, business, education, media, government, celebration, and family.

Christians make a greater impact on the world spiritually while working together. "They will know us by our love for each other."

Application

Pray for God's heart, and whether he wants to change our thinking on how to work together in the Kingdom of God.

Make a list a people you know, either in the business sphere or the ministry sphere, and write down ways you can partner in a new way to demonstrate the love and power of God to the lost.

Read and study marketplace ministry books and materials on the seven spheres of influence.

Conclusion
Kevin Stark

I wanted to write the conclusion of *Warriors Arise* while I was in my favorite nation in the world: Israel. As I start to write this, I am sitting on top of the Mount of Olives in Jerusalem. Israel is the nation of many great warriors such as David, Joshua, Daniel, Jeremiah, Ruth, Esther, and Deborah. It is a great setting to write the conclusion of a book dedicated to God and His modern-day warriors of faith.

I love the story of David's mighty men. These were the unknown warriors willing to die for an unpopular cause. The story of Stephen is also a favorite—the no-name preacher who served tables by day, and preached the gospel by night. His boldness to tell this story cost him his life, and he became the first martyr of the New Testament.

The warrior Saul, who became Paul on the road to Damascus, inspires me by the transformative power of the cross. The murderer of Christians became the voice of Christ to the Gentiles, and author of half of the New Testament.

Warriors are made, not born. The warrior Rehab was a prostitute who risked her life to help strangers because she knew it was the right thing to do. Her faith gained her safe passage out of Jericho when its walls crumbled, and now she holds a permanent place in the pages of Hebrews in the great Hall of Faith.

What I notice about warriors of the faith is that they were mostly nameless, faceless nobodies, going nowhere, that were touched by the hand of God. After His touch, they become history-makers and world-changers with a new identity and purpose. Warriors of the faith are men like John Lemmon, Rudy Valle, David Cole, and women like Karen Anderson, Sandra Kenney, and Jenny Mollison. Most of you have never heard of these people, but they are making their mark on eternity through "xtreme" love and a simple message of good news. They are changing the world.

The book of Hebrews in the New Testament has a list of warriors who did something extraordinary for God. Their only common trait was their willingness to take a risk and to follow the truth, even though the truth often goes against what seems to be the place of reason, and enters into an unknown kingdom led by a known God. To gain entry into this kingdom, you must enter through a narrow gate. Once you enter you will discover the keys to life and death.

Most of us want to play it safe in life. We want all of our ducks in a row—we want to get ready, get set, and then GO. However, the Kingdom of God is an upside-down kingdom. Often we are called to go, then get set, and finally to get ready.

In this Kingdom of God, you have to die to live, you have to become poor to become rich, and you have to forgive in order to be forgiven. Sounds strange, but that's the way this kingdom works.

In this warrior's journey, you know that God is sovereign and in control of everything, but it seems like you are in control of God's controls. Before you shout "blasphemy", hear me out: as you move, God moves. As you pray, things change. As you dream, things are set in motion.

Obviously, God is sovereign. He can do anything He wants at any time He wants to do it, but in this Kingdom of God, He has chosen to work in partnership with us. He invites us to walk with Him and to work with Him. It seems absurd that the creator of the universe would want to partner with us, not worth much more than finite grains of sand. However, as we discover the revelation of the spirit of adoption we have—and the authority we have as sons and daughters of the King—everything changes.

As you consider accepting the call to be a warrior for God, you will have to count the cost. Let me put it as clearly as possible: IT WILL COST YOU EVERYTHING. However, you will gain more than you could ever give up. You will be tested on this decision many times, and you will continually be saying yes to the will of God, until you have nothing else to say yes to.

In our journey with Team Xtreme, we have had the honor to run with many great warriors in the faith—mighty men and women of God who have counted the cost and have said yes to the call. We have also had the privilege to be under servant leaders such as Mark Anderson, Loren Cunningham, and Mike Bickle, who have demonstrated a fasted lifestyle and led us with humility and faithfulness. Through God's grace, and a wonderful family, I have learned how to fight the good fight of faith—to run with the understanding that this is a race of endurance and not a sprint. Through God's presence, obedience, humility, and love, I have learned how to run; and at other times, how to wait on the Lord. With many failures, tests, and sacrifices, my hope one day is to stand before the Lord and hear the words, "Well done, good and faithful servant."

I hope, as you have worked through this book, that you have discovered God's endless love for you. He is interested in you as a lover, not a Kingdom worker. I hope you have found humor, been challenged, encouraged, and set free by our stories. I hope these stories will serve to show that the men and women of Team Xtreme are truly only weak, ordinary people who are serving an extraordinary God.

The Team Xtreme story is just beginning, and we are believing for a new wave of warriors to be raised up from every tongue, every tribe, and every nation, who will move in a supernatural power like we have never seen before. They will believe God for whole nations; they will experience revival as an everyday occurrence; they will view days in which people are not raised from the dead as rare exceptions. This new breed of warriors will welcome sacrifice, be at home with the impossible, and will not have the word "comfortable" in their vocabulary. They will know no limits and see no faults, but live and breathe the will of God, super-charged by the Holy Spirit.

The Lord is looking for warrior men and women for His army. This is a volunteer army whose members will train you, love you, empower you, and help you to fulfill your destiny.

On New Year's Eve in 1983, I was in Kansas City, Missouri, at an event put on by Campus Crusade for Christ (now known as Cru), called "KC '83". At the end of the event, Bill Bright (Founder and President of Campus Crusade) stood up and challenged the student audience to surrender all, and to join God's army. I was deeply touched at the event. I committed my life to serve God, to do whatever He asked me to do, and to go wherever He asked me to go. I wrote out the commitment in my Bible, and started to live it out.

Many years later, again on New Year's Eve, I was at another conference in the same building called the One Thing Conference. On the way to the meeting, I grabbed an old Bible from my house and headed out the door, unaware of the sovereign moment God had in store for me. As the evening went on, I opened the front of my old Bible and was shocked to find my original GO commitment that I had not seen in years. As I looked at the date on the top of the page, I realized it was 25 years to the day that I signed my name to follow God's call for my life. I felt like God was simply saying to me, "Well done." My heart swelled with joy, thanksgiving, and excitement, as tears rolled down my cheeks.

As if that wasn't enough encouragement, to top everything off, Mike Bickle (Founder and Director of the International House of Prayer) stood up at the end of the night and challenged the student audience to surrender all, and join God's army. He also encouraged the older troops to re-enlist. Just like I had done 25 years before, I said, "Yes, Sir!" I signed up, and once again began to walk it out.

As a fitting close for this book, I have reproduced the original challenge from Bill Bright, with a place for you to sign up. I know that if you say "yes", you will never regret it, and your life will be filled with God's fullness and His awesome plans for you.

Letter from Bill Bright, 1983

The time is now.

Heavenly Father, the time is now. I have been letting encumbrances hold me back in all that I could be for You. Today, I release those things holding me back, by the power and glory of Jesus Christ. Jesus, I am ready to go and do whatever is Your will. Give me the strength to shout out, "Let your will be done! Not my will but your will!"

The harvest is plentiful but the workers are few. Lord, send me out to the harvest. Teach me to be a servant of God, one who has the courage of Esther, and the character of Daniel—one who never compromises their faith, only by Your grace.

Because of you,

Sign your name

Welcome to the world of the warrior, and to the war. "Be strong and of good courage, and do not be afraid, nor dismayed, for the Lord God is with you wherever you go." Joshua 1:9

Made in the USA
Monee, IL
24 November 2021

82818118R00095